S0-BDP-654

EVERY MAN WANTED HER

It was in this moment of innocent intimacy that Alex, standing across the room, caught sight of her. His breath snagged in his throat.

It was her. Willa. An incredible Willa. A small, voluptuous goddess. The marble statues were pale imitations next to her warmth and vitality. Her red hair glittered with golden sparks. Her enticing, diminutive figure aroused his senses. He wanted to scoop her up and carry her away.

Damn their eyes! Every man in the room was leering at her. He took a deep breath and drained his glass of woefully weak punch.

What had come over him that he should feel possessive?

BOOK YOUR PLACE ON OUR WEBSITE AND MAKE THE READING CONNECTION!

We've created a customized website just for our very special readers, where you can get the inside scoop on everything that's going on with Zebra, Pinnacle and Kensington books.

When you come online, you'll have the exciting opportunity to:

- View covers of upcoming books
- Read sample chapters
- Learn about our future publishing schedule (listed by publication month *and author*)
- Find out when your favorite authors will be visiting a city near you
- Search for and order backlist books from our online catalog
- Check out author bios and background information
- Send e-mail to your favorite authors
- Meet the Kensington staff online
- Join us in weekly chats with authors, readers and other guests
- Get writing guidelines
- AND MUCH MORE!

Visit our website at
http://www.kensingtonbooks.com

MISTAKEN KISS

Kathleen Baldwin

ZEBRA BOOKS
Kensington Publishing Corp.
www.kensingtonbooks.com

ZEBRA BOOKS are published by

Kensington Publishing Corp.
850 Third Avenue
New York, NY 10022

Copyright © 2005 by Kathleen Baldwin

All rights reserved. No part of this book may be reproduced in any form or by any means without the prior written consent of the Publisher, excepting brief quotes used in reviews.

If you purchased this book without a cover you should be aware that this book is stolen property. It was reported as "unsold and destroyed" to the Publisher and neither the Author nor the Publisher has received any payment for this "stripped book."

All Kensington titles, imprints and distributed lines are available at special quantity discounts for bulk purchases for sales promotion, premiums, fund-raising, educational or institutional use.

Special book excerpts or customized printings can also be created to fit specific needs. For details, write or phone the office of the Kensington Special Sales Manager: Kensington Publishing Corp., 850 Third Avenue, New York, NY 10022. Attn. Special Sales Department. Phone: 1-800-221-2647.

Zebra and the Z logo Reg. U.S. Pat. & TM Off.

First Printing: January 2005
10 9 8 7 6 5 4 3 2 1

Printed in the United States of America

1

Three Blind Men Stumbled Upon a Maiden

Wilhemina sat in Sir Daniel Braeburn's carriage, an object of study for the two men seated across from her.

She glanced out the window in a vain attempt to ignore them. The landscape outside jounced past in a blur of green and gray. Soon, she must convince her brother to take her to London for new spectacles. What a grand adventure they would have. If she planned very carefully she might be able to persuade him to take her to Madame Tussaud's, or perhaps even the Royal Opera House. Willa sighed deeply.

She mapped out a strategy, devised the most convincing approach, and mentally calculated the cost of such a trip. All the while paying no heed to their hushed conversation until her brother's consternation reached a crescendo.

"You see what I mean?" Jerome's voice bore tragic undertones.

Sir Daniel peered at Wilhemina suspiciously. The

coach went over a bump, and his eyes opened wide in alarm as her traitorous bosom bounced in response.

"Oh dear. I see what you mean."

Jerome slapped his hand against his thigh like a judge pronouncing sentence. "She's a full-grown female, isn't she?"

Wilhemina wanted to chide him for behaving like a dolt, but that wouldn't do, because Sir Daniel wore precisely the same absurd expression of anxiety. She squinted, trying to bring into clear focus his mouth, rounded into an alarmed O between his lamb chop side whiskers.

Sir Daniel nodded. "I'm afraid so. What are you going to do with her now?"

Jerome shook his head dolefully.

Good grief, one would think she had the plague.

She smiled at them genially. "Perhaps you ought to consider auctioning me off to the nearest traveling carnival. Judging by your conversation, I must be the only female in all of Christendom to have reached maturity. Surely, that should be worth a sovereign or two?"

The two bachelors looked at each other, their mutual fear of the female world apparent in their dour countenances.

Jerome sighed and bowed his head. "I suppose there is nothing else for it, but what I must take her to London for a Season. Though how I will stand the expense of a town house, I don't know."

Daniel clucked his tongue. "The town house is just the beginning, Jerome." He ticked off each expense on his fingers. "You must pay the earth for gowns and a party. Then, there is a chaperone to hire. I daresay your pockets will be let before the first month is out. And then, after your tremendous outlay—" He took a deep breath. "There is the unhappy possibility that Willa won't take. She's a well-enough-looking young woman, no doubt. However, I'm not at all certain spectacles and red hair are in vogue."

Jerome moaned and leaned back in the seat. His wide-brimmed hat flipped up as it knocked against the back of the carriage. He whisked it off, slapped it onto the seat, and glared at the offending female across from him.

Wilhemina's head began to hurt. She loved her brother and Sir Daniel dearly, but this entire discussion was complete and utter twaddle. "Really, you two, it's bad enough you discuss me as if I'm not here. Now, you must spout nonsense. After the training you've both given me, after forcing Greek philosophers down my throat from the time I was old enough to read, after history lessons, mathematics, and the classics—now you plan on puffing me off like any ordinary female? What an absurd notion."

Sir Daniel sat up and nudged Jerome. "I have it! My dear fellow, she's right. The solution is obvious. Why, nothing could be simpler."

Her brother perked up. "Speak man. What is it?"

"Haven't we brought her up to be nearly as engaging company to us, as we are to one another? Yes. Well, then, that's our answer. I shall marry her." He levied each point in seesaw gestures and ended by handing them his conclusion like a chef presenting them with a brilliantly decorated cake. No amorous notions. No undercurrent of desire. He simply offered them a well-reasoned solution.

Willa sighed heavily, earnestly wishing she'd chosen a different frock that morning.

Jerome closed his gaping jaw and blinked at his friend. "Marriage? You can't be serious?"

"And why not? If Willa marries me, you are spared the expense of a Season. And the three of us are free to go on just as we always have."

"You would do such a thing?"

"Of course. Haven't I known her since she was in leading strings? Nothing could be more natural. I daresay, she's the only female I'm entirely comfortable with. She'll make an admirable wife. Able to hold her own in any discussion. What possible objection can there be?"

What indeed?

Slowly, both men turned to Willa and grimaced. She glared at them as if they had completely lost their senses. In the ensuing silence, just when she needed to feel at her most imperious, she felt her old-fashioned sausage curls springing ridiculously as the coach rolled along the bumpy road to Sir Daniel's house.

Jerome cleared his throat. "Willa, my poppet, did you hear? Sir Daniel has just offered for you."

Each creak and rattle of the carriage seemed exaggerated in the uncomfortable silence. Willa opened her mouth to speak, but nothing came out. She snapped it shut, tilted her head, and reevaluated the situation. Folding her hands squarely in her lap, she refused to give rise to their preposterous suggestion.

Instead, she took another tack. "I am not your poppet. A poppet is a small child, or a little girl. You have concluded this very day that I am no longer either one; ergo, you cannot call me *your poppet.*"

"Wilhemina, be sensible. We are not debating terminology. We're discussing your future. Sir Daniel has just made a most magnanimous offer. What is your answer?"

Daniel cleared his throat. He removed his hat and

peeked sheepishly at Willa, but his words were for her brother. "I suppose, regardless of everything we've taught her, Willa is still a romantical sort of female. Perhaps we, er . . . I should've asked her on bended knee with some sort of posy in my hand." He scratched at his curly side whiskers. "A thousand pardons, my dear. Perhaps you will allow me to pay my addresses at a later date?"

The kindness in his voice never failed to soften Willa's heart. His brown eyes wavered with uncertainty and he looked, for all the world, like a forlorn puppy.

"Think carefully, Willa," chimed in Jerome. "Consider all sides of the matter before you make an answer." It was his clerical voice, a voice she had obeyed since before she could remember.

The pressure on her temples tightened. It had been a long day. Jerome's sermon had droned on for longer than usual. She'd envied those who had the luxury of nodding off to sleep in church. Willa would not dream of wounding her brother by failing to pay attention. So, she had pinched herself and sat bolt upright on the hard pew, to maintain her concentration.

And now, she was bouncing toward Sir Daniel's house for their customary Sunday nuncheon, while they stared at her, waiting anxiously for an answer that would alter her future forever, whilst maintaining theirs in perfect equilibrium.

She rubbed her throbbing forehead. "Very well. I will *consider* discussing this at another time."

"Excellent. That's settled." Jerome clapped his hands together and smiled. "Now then, Daniel, what do you say to this morning's sermon?"

Sir Daniel steepled his fingers into a perfect arch and launched into a debate over this morning's precepts. It was their favorite game, verbal chess. But today, Willa ignored them and watched the colors gallop past the window.

The coach rolled to a stop in front of Sir Daniel's manor. Willa stepped out of the carriage, missed the bottom step, and would have tumbled to the ground had not her brother caught her with one hand, and set her to rights, accomplished without so much as a pause in his conversation.

The butler held open the front doors as the gentlemen passed by, still deeply engaged in verbal combat.

"Ahem." The man attempted to attract his master's attention. "Sir Daniel, if I might have a word, a matter of some importance. We have an unexpected—"

Sir Daniel, too engrossed in his argument with Vicar Linnet, waved him off.

Wilhemina trailed behind them, completely forgotten. She stopped at the stairs and spoke loudly to their backs. "I would like to lie down, if you don't mind. I have the megrims."

Reminded of her presence, the gentlemen turned.

"Yes. Of course." Sir Daniel tapped his forehead lightly as if trying to remember what was called for in this situation. Finally, he motioned to his butler. "See to Miss Linnet's comfort." Daniel smiled uneasily at Willa. "Perhaps, we might have our little discussion later, when you are feeling more the thing."

She nodded and started up the stairs, running her hand along the banister. These stairs, which she had run up and down since childhood, now looked so different to her. They might, one day, be her stairs. Willa had never realized what a narrow hallway the house possessed. It really was a gloomy old box. The ancient house had never bothered her before. *Before,* it was simply Sir Daniel's house. Now, it might be hers forever, a dark, crumbling dungeon.

Jerome and Daniel resumed their debate and disappeared into the study, shutting the door in the butler's face. The servant sighed and turned to follow Miss Linnet up the stairs.

Willa lay down on a massive old Elizabethan bed with a cool cloth on her forehead. Would Sir Daniel do husbandly things to her here on this bed? The thought made her stomach lurch uncomfortably.

She stared at the walls, covered with a blue and white pattern she knew from memory, but could not distinguish at this distance, and tried to envision herself as his wife.

All too easy to picture, the vision was not of an altered future, but an extension of the past eighteen years. Sir Daniel was right. If she married him, the three of them would continue on just as before. There would be no romance, no adventure, no excitement, just antiquity, and books, and years and years of tired old arguments between her brother and her husband. She couldn't do it. She couldn't.

"What choice do I have?" Willa asked the musty room.

She imagined herself standing next to the beautiful debutantes who undoubtedly floated gracefully through every London Season. Her image of frilly white princesses turned sour, as she thought of how they would surely snub her, sneer at her unruly red hair, and laugh at her severe nearsightedness. With scarcely a groat to her name, no gentleman of the *ton* would stoop to marry an ill-favored miss who was nothing more than a vicar's younger sister. True, her father had been the third son of a viscount—but what was that to anything? The facts were obvious. Her chances on the marriage mart were nil.

Willa sat up and threw the cloth to the floor. "Blast it all!" She glanced defiantly at the blue walls, daring them to cave in on her for her expletive. She pulled on her kid slippers and paced up and down the ancient wooden floor.

There must be options. She could become a governess. Although, she'd spent her entire life in the schoolroom, and another twenty years might suffocate her entirely. She might become a housekeeper, but who would hire a nearly blind servant? Her shoulders slumped.

She bent down to pick up the wet cloth from the floor and caught a glimpse of herself in the oval mirror on the dressing table. She sighed and moved closer, so that her nose almost touched the glass. All she could see were her blue eyes made garishly large by the thick lenses in her spectacles. She took them off and whispered, "At least the freckles are fading."

Willa ran a finger over her lips. "Perhaps Sir Daniel has a secret passionate nature." *It must be well hidden,* she thought, *because I have never seen it.*

Marriage might be bearable if he harbored unspoken yearnings for her. She'd read of such things, unrequited passions, long-held desires. If he did, indeed, feel genuine warmth toward her, life with him might not be so wretchedly dull after all. She leaned away from the mirror and speculated on exactly how one goes about uncovering a hidden passion.

What if I were to kiss him? Surely then, I would find out if he concealed any such feelings. I might also discover whether such an activity would ignite any enthusiasm within me. A perfectly logical plan, she congratulated herself.

She looked at the face in the mirror. "It's settled then. You must kiss Sir Daniel."

Her image shook her head in refusal.

"Yes. You must do it, no matter how awkward or uncomfortable it may seem."

She grimaced at the thought, and put her glasses back on. *If he responds warmly, I suppose I ought to agree to this absurdly convenient marriage.*

Suddenly the room felt very small. "And if he doesn't—I vow, I'd rather die a spinster, and lead the apes into hell." Willa spun around and headed for the door.

She left the house through the back hall and tromped out into the Braeburn gardens. A bracing walk would bolster her courage. She set a brisk pace for herself.

Sir Daniel's gardens were a study in efficiency. Willa marched past eel ponds, past feeder streams stocked with trout, past three rows of experimental sugar beets, seven varieties of leeks, twelve strains of peas, and headed for the orchard.

The orchard was Willa's favorite haunt on Sir Daniel's grounds. The huge old nut trees grew in cheerful disarray, and there was a small Greek folly hidden in their midst. Here and there Daniel's grandfather had placed wooden benches around the tree trunks. No matter how much Daniel tried to groom the natural appearance out of it, the grove remained an inviting and comfortable refuge.

Willa slowed her steps and squinted up at the canopy of branches overhead. She could not see details, but the trees formed a ceiling of shifting colors and muted light, wonderful flickering patterns—light against dark, dark against light.

She lowered her gaze and connected with a shape that was foreign to the grove. Straining to make sense of it, Willa moved slowly toward the dark shape.

It appeared to be a man slouched on a bench, relaxing against a tree trunk, with his long legs unceremoniously sprawled out. She squinted, and then caught her breath as she recognized Daniel.

This is beyond good fortune. No sooner had she decided what course of action must be taken, than God had delivered the opportunity into her hands.

Willa straightened her shoulders and flexed her hands at her sides. *Courage,* she commanded herself. *Your entire future is at stake. It must be done. Kiss him.*

She charged forward. Halfway there, she stopped, remembering the garishly big eyes staring back at her from the mirror, and removed her glasses. She meant to make this moment as perfect as possible. With that thought, she stuffed the spectacles into her pocket and proceeded on with her campaign.

Willa tripped on a fallen branch lying on the ground in front of him. Recovering her composure, she faced her quarry squarely. He did not look up. She cleared her throat and waited for the blurry face to respond. He remained motionless.

"Ahem. Pardon me, for intruding on you in this manner. But these are most fortuitous circumstances. I have a request of a delicate nature to ask of you. Before I make a decision regarding your generous offer of marriage, I wish for you to kiss me."

There was no answer. "To see if we will suit, of course. Perfectly logical."

When he still did not respond she moved closer, so close she could smell the faint scent of shaving soap and brandy. "Please, sir. I know it is highly irregular, but would you *please* kiss me?" Willa put one tentative hand on his shoulder, leaned her face toward his, and closed her eyes.

When he heard the voice, Alexander Braeburn stirred in his slumber. Exhausted from having ridden the entire night, he was having a particularly effective dream. A shapely young maiden was demanding to be kissed.

She thrust her face toward his and he could almost feel her warm breath. Her hair was the color of spice and her skin was creamy, with just enough freckles to convince one of her innocence. A dream like this must not be denied. He caught the face in his hands and kissed it with enthusiasm.

When the curvaceous dream whispered, "Oh my." Alex laughed, a drowsy, husky chuckle. He pulled the dream across his lap and kissed her again. The noise from his own throat propelled Alexander to complete consciousness, that, and the superb reality of the mouth he was kissing.

This was no dream, no matter how exhausted he might be. Her lips were full and sensuous, and they yielded to his in a way that sent currents of heat through his loins. He looked down into the young woman's wide blue eyes.

Willa's mind turned to thick jelly. Kissing was tenfold better than she had imagined. Joy flooded through her veins. Life with him was going to be wonderful.

She blinked up at his face and squinted. She raised her hand to his cheek and stroked the clean-shaven skin. "You have no side whiskers."

"No." It was half spoken, half whispered, but Willa instantly knew the voice was not Sir Daniel's.

"You're not Daniel."

"No."

She did not leap out of his lap. He did not remove his hand from her waist.

"Oh. Then, it would seem, I've kissed you by mistake." She spoke slowly, trying to keep the mournful tenor she felt out of her speech.

"Apparently." His voice gathered more fullness, a soothing baritone with undertones that made her think he was suppressing laughter.

"It was most enjoyable." She tried to smile, acting as if it were a trifle.

"Thank you."

"Is kissing always so pleasant?" She squinted up at him, trying to read his expression, falling prey to the compelling lines of his jaw and the mouth that had so effectively kissed hers.

Alex nodded. "Yes, generally. But, not always quite so—" He almost told her that kissing did not usually set him on fire this quickly. "I cannot answer your question."

She slid off his lap, took her glasses out of her pocket, put them on her nose, studying him, as if she were the local magistrate interrogating a poacher. "You look very like Sir Daniel. Who are you?"

Alex smiled. She wore her hair in an ancient style, her blue eyes were enormous behind the lenses, and her clothing was from another age. "I am his brother, Alexander Braeburn, at your service."

"Of course, now I remember. There's a painting in the hall of him standing with a younger brother. He never speaks of you."

"I'm not surprised."

"You don't visit often, or I would have known you."

"A logical deduction." He smiled.

She sighed wearily. "Yes. I am nothing, if not logical."

"You appear to be many things. *Logical* would not have ranked high on the list I was composing. Do you have a name?"

"Miss Linnet, Wilhemina Linnet. However, in view of the fact that I have already taken the liberty of kissing you, you may call me Willa."

"Ah, Linnet. I know the name. Surely you cannot be the vicar's little sister? You're all grown up."

She frowned. "So it would seem."

He remained seated and lazily bowed his head. "A privilege. Am I to understand that you thought you were kissing my brother?"

Willa pressed her lips together and nodded. "I was testing him."

"Testing?" One of Alex's eyebrows shot up.

"Yes, to ascertain if he had a passion in him for anything besides intellectual pursuits. I cannot marry him without some passion."

Alex struggled to remain solemn. "I see."

"It isn't a laughing matter, sir. I am quite undone. For his kisses will certainly never compare to yours. Now, I must spend the rest of my life with the unhappy knowledge that there are better kisses to be had."

Alex folded his arms across his chest and grinned at the young woman standing beguilingly between his legs, without the least awareness of her effect on him. "Perhaps you are mistaken about that."

She shook her head. "I doubt it."

"A great logician like yourself must surely spy the solution?"

"There is none. No. It's a futile undertaking." Her chest heaved gravely.

Such a serious maiden. He was almost moved to compassion over her nonsensical dilemma. "Why not complete your plan? Kiss him, as you did me. If you find Daniel as passionless as you fear, simply refuse to marry him." He shrugged. "It isn't so difficult."

"Naturally, I've already weighed that course of action."

Willa studied Alex. His features were the mirror image of Daniel's, and yet on this man the curly brown hair invited her to run her fingers through it. The hard plains of his jaw were tempered with smile lines, and he had a dimple next to his mouth. The brown eyes flashed with merriment, and his brows were not so heavy as his brother's. Small distinctions, yet they made a world of difference.

She shook her head. "You haven't considered the consequences." Mimicking her brother's teaching tone, she continued. "Suppose I kiss Sir Daniel, find him lacking, and therefore, do not marry. Then, I must spend the rest of my days as a spinster, with *no* kisses at all."

"An unhappy alternative."

"Yes." She shifted closer to him. "After today, it is unthinkable. I wonder if I might impose upon you to kiss me once more? So that I may remember it well?"

He arched one brow. "Are you sure it is wise?"

"No. It is, undoubtedly, unwise. Wholly improper. But when I am old and alone, I would like to be able to look back on such an experience. As a gentleman, you cannot deny me this simple request."

"How old are you? All of sixteen years I would guess."

"No, of course not. I am one score and eight. You probably miscalculated because I am so short."

"I see. Eighteen. In that case, given the prospect of

your dotage, it's almost a deathbed request. How can I refuse?" He inclined his head with a flourish. "Your servant."

She leaned closer to him. "I'll remove my spectacles, if you like. When I'm this close, I assure you I can see fairly well."

"You must please yourself." He stood up to perform his duty.

She folded her glasses carefully and placed them in her pocket. Nervously, she leaned up on her toes, closing the distance between them.

Alex didn't grab her as he had before. He bent his head, letting her come to him and timidly place her lips on his. When she pressed her full lips against his, he opened his mouth and coaxed her into a deeper kiss. He touched her waist, lightly tracing the old-fashioned cinched waist, enjoying the narrowness. Then he flattened his hand against her back and pulled her to him. She yielded, melting into his embrace, pouring fire into his veins.

Alex took a breath and forced himself to let go. It was time to stop, or the delightful Miss Linnet would soon discover what followed kisses.

She remained close enough that her breath tickled his chin when she spoke. "Thank you. I will never forget that."

Alex grinned lopsidedly. "I assure you, Miss Linnet, I will not soon forget it either. Now, perhaps it is time we went back to the house."

He wondered, briefly, what possessed him. Why should he behave with such restraint on her behalf? Wasn't she offering, nay, begging, for him to kiss her? If she relished kissing so much, wouldn't she also enjoy . . . but no, she was after all an innocent, the vicar's little sister.

Willa set her spectacles back on her nose. They strolled silently through the grove of trees until she turned and looked up at Alex. "Are you a rake? Is that why Daniel never speaks of you? Is that why you kiss so wonderfully well?"

"I've been called many things, let me see—a wastrel, a scapegrace, a prodigal, a gamester—but no, I can't recall being designated a rake."

Willa was quiet for a moment. "Oh, but surely, most wastrels and gamesters are rakes as well."

Alex was unable to keep from smiling at her audacity. "I bow to your superior knowledge of the breed."

Willa huffed. "Now you are gammoning me, Mr. Braeburn."

"Alex." He corrected her.

"Very well, Alex. Why does Daniel never speak of you?"

Alex glanced down at the headstrong imp walking next to him. "I did mention *prodigal* in that list of traits, did I not? Well, there you have it. I was expelled from Eton. Tormented a score of England's finest tutors. Had no interest in experimenting with leeks. And apparently had a talent for getting into mischief. Daniel and Father decided I was an embarrassment to the Braeburn name. My father bought me an officer's commission, to which I was wholly unsuited. I sold out two years later. That was the *coup de grace.*"

"What about your mother?"

"You ask very pointed questions for a young lady."

"Nonsense. I merely wish to know what your mother thought of all this. If I were a mother, I would not expect all my children to be the same. That would be rather like expecting a cabbage to be a melon." Willa pointed toward the garden.

"A cabbage. I'm flattered, Miss Linnet."

"I did not mean—"

He held up his hand to forestall her apology. "Quite right. I was a cabbage in the melon patch. Fortunately, my mother was rather fond of cabbage. You see, she could hunt and jump as well as any man. It was she who taught me to ride. For my tenth birthday she gave me a hunter, a mare with an excellent bloodline."

Alex turned his gaze toward the stables. It was an unconscious movement, followed by an unchecked wince of pain.

"What happened? Did the horse die?"

"No." He looked straight ahead. "Mother died the following year. Father sold off everything in the stable except for his coaching teams."

"Even your hunter?"

"Yes, Miss Inquisitive, even my mare. It was not necessary for my education."

"How could he have been so heartless?" Willa looked up at him with eyes full of compassion.

"Not heartless. Practical. It costs a great deal to keep a horse of that sort."

"Hhmm. Nevertheless, I think it is unconscionable that Daniel does not speak of you."

"You're too hard on him. You forget the private tutors I ran through, the cost of a commission. And as I mentioned, I do not care for endless book reading, nor experimental farming. No, I'm contented to stay away." Alex gestured toward the garden rows labeled with cards on stakes. "I'm not a farmer, nor a squire by nature. Daniel thinks of me as a gambler. I prefer to call myself a sporting man. We have very little in common. I suspect that he does not mention me simply because he does not think of me. Nor do I think of him often."

Willa tilted her head. "Yet, you are here, visiting your brother."

Alex laughed. "A matter of convenience, Miss Linnet. There is a prizefight between a London fellow and a bruising country lad. It takes place tomorrow afternoon, just outside St. Cleve. I'm simply imposing on my brother's hospitality until the contest is over."

"I see." Willa bit her bottom lip. "And you have a wager on one of these fellows?"

"Of course."

"Which one did you place your bet on? The London fellow, or the country lad?"

Alex adjusted the lace at his sleeve. "Well, Miss Inquisitive, I will make it a game for you. You must figure it out for yourself, and I'll tell you if you guess correctly."

"Oh, but this is too easy." Willa grinned at him. "You've placed your bet on the London man, and I will tell you why. You think our local boy will be a great slow lummox and the London chap is a more sophisticated pugilist. Am I right?"

"Why, Miss Linnet, you astound me." He bowed. "And do you concur?"

"That depends on who the country lad is. Tell me the fellow's name, so I may decide."

"Ah, but then you'll have an unfair advantage."

"Do you mean to tell me you know nothing of the fighter from London?"

He laughed. "You don't miss a step do you?"

"Unfortunately, I miss quite a few. I need new eyeglasses. But that is beside the point. Who is the fellow from St. Cleve?"

"The young man's name is George Thompson."

"Georgie? Oh, but you must be mistaken. Georgie is hardly a grown man. Why, George Thompson is only seventeen. It cannot be."

"I'm certain of the name. Perhaps there are two George Thompsons in the neighborhood. It is a common-enough name."

"Yes, there are two, but the other is young George's father. And I can assure you, Mr. Thompson is not a boxer."

Alex held out his hands. "I don't know what to say. It must be your Georgie. Seventeen is not so very young. There are boys much younger fighting for their king and country on the Continent."

"But he's needed on their farm. If anything should happen to him, I don't know how his father will get on." Willa frowned and kicked at a stone. The stone proved too large for her slippered foot to stir. She winced and hopped on the other leg.

Alex held out his arm, she took it and limped along next to him.

"Where is this contest to be held?" she asked in an irritated clip.

"I believe Lord Winthrop has volunteered one of his tenants' pastures, north of town."

"Oh lovely, now the poor tenant's pasture will be trampled by spectators from London."

"Surely, the man will be paid."

"I certainly hope so. But, that says nothing to the fact that poor Georgie will have his head bashed in by your vicious London man."

"Then you believe my wager is well placed."

"How can you consider the money, sir? This is barbaric. What pleasure can you have watching two men thrash each other as if they were recalcitrant schoolboys?"

"It is a great mystery," he said with false gravity. Then Alex stopped abruptly and turned to her. "I don't suppose there is any chance this Georgie fellow has paid a visit to Gentleman Jackson's Pugilist Academy in London?"

"That's ridiculous. He's never left the farm."

Alex clicked his tongue and shook his head, but walked on with a smug grin.

"You may gloat, Mr. Braeburn. But I assure you something will be done. You will not win any money on *this* contest. This massacre will never take place—not if I have to stop it myself!"

To which Alex's shoulders shook with merriment. "My dear Miss Linnet, what a perfectly terrifying female you are." He could hold back no longer and laughed out loud.

Willa let go of his arm, tilted her chin into the air, and marched off in a great hurry toward the house. Alex stopped and, with pleasant speculation, watched her hips swing, without artifice, from side to side as she stomped resolutely away. *Intriguing little minx.*

Willa vowed to herself she would show Alex she meant what she said. But first she would prove that she was right about Sir Daniel. It was time to settle the matter of her engagement. She proceeded directly down the hallway, and thrust open the study door. There they sat, Jerome and Daniel, still engaged in the same heated debate.

"I might've known," she muttered. In a considerably sterner tone she addressed her brother. "Jerome, I would like a few moments alone with Sir Daniel."

"Not now, Willa, I—" Jerome took one look at her and appeared to reconsider.

Willa shut the door behind her brother and marched up to Daniel. "Kiss me, Daniel."

He sprang to his feet and shuffled uncomfortably. Sir Daniel's face turned red and then white. He fidgeted with his cuffs. "Really, Willa, what can you mean?"

"It's quite simple. I mean for you to kiss me."

Daniel coughed and pulled at his collar. "I'm not at all sure it's proper, perhaps after we are married—"

Willa stamped her foot. "Perhaps? *Perhaps,* you will suffer a kiss after we are married? Daniel, you will kiss me now, or there will *be* no marriage."

He studied the corners of his ceiling. His fingers were no longer steepled in a perfectly matching arch. They fumbled together, twisting and wringing into a knot.

"Very well." He closed his eyes, bent toward Willa's upturned face and planted a small kiss on her forehead.

"That is not what I meant." Willa pointed to her lips.

Daniel stumbled backward and bumped into a bookcase.

She stepped toward him.

His eyes no longer looked like those of a sad puppy. They reminded Willa of a frightened hare.

"It doesn't hurt," she tried to persuade him.

Daniel straightened his shoulders, and for a moment he resembled Alex. "Really, Willa, this is all quite peculiar. You have never behaved in this manner toward me before."

"You've never offered marriage to me before. If you won't kiss me, simply withdraw your proposal."

"I can't do that. A matter of honor, don't you see? What would your brother think?"

"Are you going to kiss me, or not?"

"Yes. Yes, very well." He closed his eyes, puckered his lips and slumped toward her. Willa pressed her mouth against his as she had done to Alex. Daniel created a small smacking noise and withdrew.

"As I thought." Willa turned around.

Alex had entered through the back of the house, and meandered down the hallway toward Daniel's study, curious as to how Miss Inquisitive's quest for passion fared. He found the vicar squatting outside the door, peering in through the keyhole. At the sound of Alex's boots clicking on the marble floor, Jerome jumped up, red-faced and stammering.

Alex chuckled. "Well met, Jerome."

Jerome gawked at him. "I don't usually . . . my sister . . ." He pointed at the door.

Alex nodded, and tried to school his features. He could well imagine Daniel quaking like a jelly as Willa made her demands. "Unusual young woman, your sister. Unless I miss my guess, she's testing my brother."

"Testing? But, but—" Jerome stuttered and appeared to be almost at the point of regaining his equilibrium when the door flew open, forcing him to leap out of the way. A set of magnified blue eyes accosted both of them.

Willa looked decidedly unhappy.

"I was right." She glared pointedly at Alex and then turned to her brother. "There will be no marriage. You may tell Sir Daniel he is off the hook. And you needn't worry about me, Jerome. I'll hie me off to a nunnery and tend the sick."

She flounced past them and headed up the stairway. Jerome followed closely on her heels. "Willa, be sensible. This is preposterous. You've been reading too much Shakespeare. Aside from that, you'll find there aren't any sick people in nunneries these days.

And as to finding a convent, well, this is England. You know full well that Queen Elizabeth—" His voice trailed off as he wound up the stairwell after her.

Alex's mouth curved up into a one-sided grin. So, the little whirlwind hadn't liked Daniel's kisses. He felt unaccountably pleased.

2

Jack Be Nimble, Jack Be Quick

I've watched the seconds pat and nurse
Their man; and seen him put to bed;
With twenty guineas in his purse,
And not an eye within his head.
J.H. Reynolds, *The Fancy*

"I kissed him."

"Never say you did, Miss Willa."

"Oh, but I did. I did, Aggie, and it was wonderful."

The candle on the vanity flickered against the darkness of night. Aggie adjusted the white mobcap atop her graying hair. Then she looked down into the mirrored reflection of her mistress's face and shook the hairbrush at her.

"No, miss. It weren't wonderful. You mustn't do such things. Gentle-bred young ladies mustn't go about kissing gentlemen. I learnt you better'n that, I did."

"Taught. You *taught* me to behave better than that."

"That's what I said. It's not ladylike."

"Well, I did kiss him. The deed is done. In fact, I liked it so much, I asked him to do it again."

Aggie squawked. Then she slapped the back of the brush against Willa's upper bottom.

"Ouch!" Willa twisted around and scowled up at Aggie. She rubbed the sting through her nightgown. "Very well, I won't tell you the rest."

"Humph." Aggie vigorously brushed through Willa's tangled curls. Willa closed her eyes and leaned back while the brush pulled roughly through her hair.

The silence only lasted a few moments before Aggie started muttering. "Sir Daniel is as fine a man as ever there was. If you was to marry him, you wouldn't never starve. A sensible girl would know where to get her bread baked."

"Buttered."

"But, no, you'd rather kiss a stranger than marry a respectable gentleman. And I ask you, what kind of man takes advantage of a green young miss like that fellow done?"

"Oh, he's completely unsuitable. A rakehell, to be sure."

Aggie whacked Willa's bottom once more. "Mind your tongue, my girl."

"Well, it's the truth. He's not the sort of gentleman who takes an interest in proper young ladies. He probably has any number of beautiful paramours. Exotic women from other countries, who put kohl on their eyes and wear silks from the Far East, and—"

"I don't want to hear no more about them fallen women. All the more reason for you to marry a good, decent and honorable—"

"I can't marry Sir Daniel."

"And why not?"

Willa cocked her head sideways and looked into the mirror. She didn't want to miss Aggie's reaction. "I kissed Sir Daniel, too. Frankly, it was as dull as old porridge."

Aggie stepped backward and dropped onto the bed. She looked at the child she had cared for since infancy and shook her head.

"Oh, Aggie, don't act so shocked. I had to know what it would be like, didn't I?"

Willa stood up and walked over to the wardrobe. "I wish I had something to wear besides Mother's old dresses." She opened the doors and plowed through the garments hanging inside. She spun around to her maid. "Which of these gowns is the most fashionable?"

There was no response. Aggie sat with her arms folded across her chest, sulking.

"Come now, Aggie, surely you can remember which of my mother's gowns was made last?"

"Of course, I do. It were the rose silk."

"It *was* the rose silk." Willa draped the skirt of the rose silk over her arm. "Hmm. Do you suppose the ladies from Town might wear silk to a prizefight?"

"I expect they might—*those* kinds of ladies. A prize-fight is no place for a gentlewoman."

"Probably not. It's just that poor little Georgie Thompson has gotten himself in a fix. I'm afraid he'll be killed if I don't do something."

"Georgie? That great bull ox? He can take care of himself."

"No, Aggie. There is a fellow, Jackson, in London who teaches brutes the art of boxing. The man who is coming is one of those trained fighters. Alex told me so. Georgie is going to get his head smashed in."

"Then you ought to tell your brother, and leave a man to straighten out things like this."

"I tried to talk to Jerome on the way home from Sir Daniel's. He refuses to speak to me until I come to my senses and agree to marry Daniel. You saw him tonight. He was stiff as stone. No, I have to do it myself." *And this way,* she thought, *I may have one last glimpse of Alex before he disappears out of my life forever.*

Aggie smacked her hand on the bed covers. "If I didn't know better I'd think you had brain fever. You can't go traipsing out into a field full of men, some of 'em strangers from London. It isn't proper. Everyone will talk."

Willa walked over to the bed and sat down. She lifted one of Aggie's hands and rubbed it against her cheek.

"Be reasonable. You know I can't let that London fellow hurt our Georgie. He's just a boy."

"He's not a boy. He's your age, my girl."

Willa exhaled loudly and let go of Aggie's hand. "Never mind that. He'll get killed if I don't do something. Don't you worry. Everyone in the village knows me. They'll realize the importance of what I'm doing. They won't let anything bad happen to me."

"You're not listening to me, Wilhemina. I see that contrite look in your eye."

"Contrite? What do you mean? Oh. You mean *contrary.*"

"I mean—you're going to land in a hay wagon full of trouble, that's what."

Willa went back to the wardrobe and studied its contents while tapping her chin with one finger.

"Do you think this rose silk will fit me?"

Aggie shook her head and sighed.

* * *

The next day, Willa, decked out in her mother's rose silk, sat in the driver's seat of a small black dog-cart and rolled slowly along the rutted road out of St. Cleve.

"Get along now, Euripides. Hurry up, I say. Oh, Euripides, you stubborn lump, at this pace we'll never get to Lord Winthrop's field by two o'clock."

She slapped the traces against the buttocks of her plump brown mule. Completely ignoring her directives, he stopped to pluck a tuft of grass from the roadside.

"You stubborn infernal beast—you're holding up traffic."

A high-perch phaeton loaded with dandies from London whipped around her. They whistled and jeered at Willa in her small buggy as they passed. Annoyed at both the rude men and her defiant animal, she smacked Euripides with her whip. Instead of moving down the road like he was supposed to, the mule's eyes widened and his back legs sprang into action. Up and down the cart went as he bucked. Willa held her glasses with one hand to keep them from flying off her nose and clutched the traces with the other, trying desperately to keep the rebellious mule from landing both of them in the ditch.

The cart spun sideways, blocking most of the road, and Euripides came to a standstill in the path of an oncoming coach. The coachman pulled his team up short to keep from smashing into them.

Willa clipped the traces, grabbed a carrot from a box under the seat (kept there for just such occasions), and went to speak with Euripides. She grasped his harness and held the carrot in front of his face. The mule walked obediently beside her, his lips rolling and curling up while his big teeth opened and shut, trying to snatch the carrot.

"Ornery animal. I don't know why Jerome keeps you. You are the most obstinate creature on God's green earth."

The fancy black carriage rolled past her. Willa spotted a blurry but elegant crest painted on the door. A red-haired lady inside the coach leaned out of the window, as if straining to get a closer look.

"What a sight we must be." Willa shoved the carrot into his greedy mouth and climbed back into her cart.

"I should have walked. It would have been faster."

Willa arrived at the prizefight with her sausage curls wilting and mud splattered on the hem of her outdated rose silk gown. Her confidence wavered as she surveyed the enormous crowd. There were more people standing in the field than ever came to church. There were more people gathered there than even the parish fair attracted.

Willa squinted, searching the crowd for familiar faces and saw none. Beautiful ladies sat in low-slung elegant carriages and atop tall phaetons. The people laughed loudly, shouted, and threw things. Girls roamed through the crowd, selling oranges from boxes hung on their hips.

In the center of it all, Willa saw Georgie standing tall and quiet, like a man waiting to be executed. She renewed her courage for his sake. Brushing a strand of unruly red hair out of her eyes, she wriggled her way through the crowd.

* * *

Alex tapped his hand on his thigh. He consulted his pocket watch and then counted the number of heads in front of him at the betting post. The fight was set to begin any minute.

After getting a good look at *little* Georgie, he wanted to hedge his bets. He knew Jack Scroggins was handy with his fives, but little Georgie looked like an overgrown fjord horse. One good blow from that farm boy and Scroggins would think he'd been hit with a sledge. Alex glanced back toward the ring to make sure he wasn't overreacting to George Thompson's size. It was then that he saw Willa—headed straight for the ropes.

Alex looked up at the heavens and shook his head. He consulted his watch again and calculated his distance from the betting post in terms of minutes. No time to do anything about a stubborn young woman, who should have stayed at home and out of trouble. The idea that she thought she needed to rescue Gigantic Georgie was ludicrous. Alex spotted her red curls just as she slipped under the cording.

"It's none of my affair," he said aloud to convince himself. "I hardly know the chit." Then he heard the laughing start. Alex clenched his teeth, inhaled deeply, turned around, and plowed through the crowd.

It wasn't easy shoving his way up toward the center of the gathering, but he persisted.

"Excuse me, I must remove that bit of baggage cluttering up the ring," he explained as he pushed through the spectators. At first they laughed and stepped aside, but as he got closer the crowd was more hostile.

He heard Willa reprimanding the gargantuan boxer. "Go home, Georgie. You might be killed or maimed if you stay here. Then what will your poor father do?"

Alex couldn't see her, but he pictured her, hands on her hips, one finger shaking imperiously at her prey. Men standing outside the ropes began to boo her.

The hulking farm boy answered his would-be rescuer. "I can't go home, Miss Willa. All these folks come here t' see me fight."

"That's not the point, George—"

"Leave the man alone!" a fellow in the front shouted.

Willa turned toward the voice. "You should all go home. This is no way for grown men to behave."

A shout went up. "Get her out of there!"

"Methodist!" Someone threw an apple core. It hit her in the shoulder. Willa ducked as a volley of fruit flew toward her. Alex stepped into the square. The mob hushed. He walked toward her, smiling broadly, holding his hand up to the crowd. For a moment, it was quiet. He bent toward her, grasped her around the waist, and hoisted her over his shoulder. Everyone burst out laughing.

A cheer went up as Alex carried her out of the ring. Spectators lowered the ropes and parted like the Red Sea. Alex carried her away to a hail of compliments.

"Well done, man." Someone patted him on his free shoulder as he passed.

"Cart her off to the asylum, lad."

Willa held on to her glasses as she flopped unceremoniously against his back. This wasn't the way she had planned it. She had hoped to meet up with him after she had stopped the fight and dispersed the crowd. This was hardly the triumph she envisioned.

Augmenting her humiliation, a brown mush of overripe pear oozed down her sleeve.

"I'm getting pear juice on your coat."

Alex tightened his grip on her thighs. She fit quite tidily on his shoulder, the little imp. "I'll send you a laundering bill."

He didn't know if he felt like flogging her or laughing at her. The fight began behind him. The crowd lost interest in Willa and started cheering for their respective champions.

He continued to haul her away from the throng. It wasn't until a parasol poked him in the midsection that he stopped.

"You will put my niece down this instant."

Alex looked at the lady in front of him. She was obviously wealthy, and had the air of a woman used to having her own way. Her hair was an unnatural shade of red and her eyes unreadable. Alex didn't trust her.

"Willa, do you know this woman?" He turned slightly. Willa twisted sideways and peered up through her smeared spectacles at the well-dressed lady in front of them.

"No." She flopped against his back.

"I," said the lady imperiously, "am the Countess de Alameda, your aunt."

Alex almost dropped his passenger, he was so surprised. He knew the lady by reputation.

Willa twisted around, wiping and adjusting her glasses. "Aunt Honore?"

"The same." She thumped the point of her parasol against the ground as if she were the queen, and it was her staff. "Now, if you will kindly set my niece on the ground."

What was the infamous Lady Alameda doing in this neighborhood? She usually ran with the Carleton crowd. How could she possibly have a niece like Willa? The two didn't belong in the same courtyard together, much less the same family tree. It didn't seem credible.

Alex smiled congenially. "As much as I would like to oblige you, Lady Alameda, I'm afraid it is out of the question."

The countess sputtered. "Of all the impudent—"

"Practical, my lady. You see, if I put her down, your niece will head straight back into the boxing arena to rescue that huge young man you see fighting in there." Alex smiled at the look on the lady's face. "Then, I will be obliged to fetch her out again. The crowd was tolerant the first time, but a second time, and in the midst of the match . . ." He shook his head.

Lady Alameda stared at Alex. "Wilhemina! Is any of this nonsense true?"

Willa, who was not at all sure she would really go running back into the ring to be pelted with fruit again, considered her answer carefully. She rather enjoyed riding around on Alex's shoulder. If he put her down, it was quite possible she might never see him again. She twisted around Alex's side while holding her glasses in place and attempted to focus through the one lens not thoroughly clouded with fruit juice.

"Highly probable. Georgie is one of our parishioners. My duty to protect him. My brother is the vicar, you see, and—"

"I know who your brother is."

A shout went up from the crowd, and Alex spun around to see what the commotion was over.

Willa thumped on his back. "What's happening? What is it? Tell me."

"It's Scroggins—he's letting it fly to Georgie's chin.

Hammering the big fellow with his famous quick punches."

Willa moaned.

Honore studied Alex and Willa. A more unlikely pair never existed. Alex was obviously a Corinthian, well dressed and worldly. Yet, here he stood with her countrified little niece slung over his shoulder. *How very intriguing.* Honore perked up like a cat that has just spotted a mouse in the kitchen.

Cheers and huzzahs rose from the crowd. Willa rapped Alex harder. "What happened?"

Alex reached up and smacked her bottom. "Scroggins won, my girl! You just saved me twenty-five pounds."

Honore raised one eyebrow after observing Alex pat her niece in such a familiar way. She cleared her throat. "The fight is over. I believe you may safely put her down."

Alex sighed involuntarily. He supposed he must. He lowered Willa down slowly, appreciating every luscious curve as she slid over his chest. He winked and smiled provocatively at her, just to vex the arrogant Lady Alameda.

Willa's face did not mirror his levity. She was troubled. "Is George dead? Can you see him?" She clung to his arm and strained on tiptoe to see over the crowd, to no avail.

Alex shook his head. "No. He's not dead. Took one to the jaw and went out like a candle. He'll come around in a moment or two."

"How can you be certain? Was he bleeding? Who's there to tend him?" Willa plunged into the crowd. "I have to see for myself." She shouted over her shoulder.

Alex shut his eyes and sighed.

Honore ground her parasol deeper into the dirt. "Do something."

"Begging your pardon, my lady, but it's none of my affair. I set her on the ground at *your* request and now—" He held his hand out toward the mob encircling the ring.

Honore narrowed her eyes at him. "You most certainly are involved, young man. Or you wouldn't have been carrying her around like a sack of potatoes?"

"I agree, a shabby practice. In the future, I promise not to rescue young ladies by slinging them over my shoulder like sacks of vegetables."

"Don't get impertinent with me. What's your name?"

"Alex Braeburn, at your service, my lady." He bowed extravagantly.

She arched one eyebrow. "I've heard of you. You're not what I pictured. Pictured someone older."

"Ah, you must be thinking of the noble *Sir Daniel Braeburn,* ma'am. I'm his younger brother—the not-so-noble."

"Hmmm. No, I don't think so. Heard something." She tapped her cheek and then waved away the annoying riddle. "It doesn't matter. Go and fetch my niece. Then, we will all retire to the vicarage for a rest and dinner." Honore produced a handkerchief and waved it in front of her face. "All this running about has tired me to the bone."

Alex frowned at Honore. She didn't look weary to him.

"Well, don't just stand there, boy. Go after her."

He inclined his head and went in search of Willa. He found her instructing George Thompson's seconds to use caution as they lifted the puffy-faced lad into the back of his father's splintered old farm wagon. Blood trickled from the poor wretch's mouth. All in all, Alex had seen far worse, particularly when Scroggins had been the other contender.

The elder Thompson said nothing. He glumly climbed up onto the creaking wooden driver's seat and grunted to his team. The wagon lurched forward, and Georgie moaned. Willa waved sadly at his retreating figure. Alex put his hand on her shoulder. "He'll be mended in a day or two."

Willa looked up at him, her spectacle-rimmed eyes brimming with concern. "I should have done something."

"You certainly tried." Alex felt an inexplicable urge to hug her to his chest and stroke his hand over her strawberry tresses. But he resisted.

She shook her head, and those ridiculous red curls fluttered like weightless springs on the breeze. "His father said I upset Georgie. That's why he lost the fight." Willa's eyes pleaded with him to tell her it wasn't so.

Alex smiled reassuringly. "No. He never stood a chance. Scroggins has been knocking out big fellows since he was a lad of twelve. There was nothing you could do."

He gave her shoulders a gentle pat. She leaned in to him, and what could he do? He comforted her briefly. Silly, he shouldn't let this wisp of a girl, in clothing she must have dragged down from the attic, affect him. His taste ran to ballerinas and widows who could fend for themselves. He let go of her and cleared his throat.

"Your aunt commissioned me to fetch you. Rather like a dog sent after a stick. Should I fail to return promptly, with you in tow, I'm mortally afraid she'll whip me across the nose with her umbrella."

He grinned and held out his arm.

Willa placed her hand on his sleeve and walked beside him, wishing desperately that she were not spattered with mud and rotten fruit.

3

Some Like It Hot, Some Like It Cold

"Aunt Honore, you cannot be serious. You can't simply give away our mule."

"Oh, but I can. I saw you struggling on the road with this deplorable animal. Good heavens, child, my coach nearly ran you over, all because of this worthless donkey. I'll give him to the first passerby, before I allow you to drive him home."

"No, my lady! My brother would have a fit. Then there is the rig to consider. How would I get it home? Pull it myself? Besides, Euripides is not a donkey. He's a mule—Jerome's mule. And considerably more expensive than a donkey."

"Bah!" Honore waved her hand in the air, erasing Willa's arguments. "Mule, donkey, who cares. I'll reimburse Jerome. He needs new equipage anyway."

Alex folded his arms across his chest and leaned against a tree while Willa argued with her aunt. Honore stabbed the air with her parasol, leveling it at a passerby, a heavyset young buck. "You there. Yes, you.

Do you see this ridiculously fat creature? I'll give you this—"

Honore indicated the mule by rapping her parasol on Euripides's backside. Willa looked from her aunt to Euripides just in time to see the beast's eyes widen and roll back in his head.

"Look out!" Willa lunged for her aunt, and pushed her out of the way. Euripides brayed and kicked up his hind legs. He whirled around, bucking in every direction. The prospective owner jumped clear of the enraged animal and walked off, shaking his head.

Honore and Willa hid behind a tree. Honore straightened up from her crouching position. "Good heavens! That demented animal nearly killed me. Shoot it."

"Nonsense! You poked him with your umbrella. He's a perfectly lovely mule, and he belongs to my brother and me. You have no right to sell him or shoot him." Willa planted her hands firmly on her hips.

"A lovely mule? *That,* my dear, is a contradiction in terms."

The beast in question stopped braying and was once again chewing contentedly on grass and weeds.

Alex approached the squabbling women and cleared his throat. "Much as I am loath to put an end to this entertaining debate, may I offer a solution?"

Both women turned to him without saying a word. Honore's eyebrows narrowed skeptically, and Willa looked at him like an expectant teacher ready to pounce if her pupil should make a wrong answer. He smiled in an obvious attempt to disarm them.

"I'll be happy to tie my mount to the rear of Miss Linnet's cart and drive her back to the vicarage. I believe I can manage the 'demented' beast." He gestured toward Euripides, grazing placidly a few feet away.

Honore's eyebrows snapped back into place. "Very well. Yes. That will answer nicely. Thank you, Mr. Braeburn, and of course, you must stay at the vicarage and dine with us."

Willa's jaw tightened as her aunt made free with the vicarage's hospitality. She thought better of it when Alex nodded his acceptance. Her face relaxed, and she could not contain the smile that spread across her features. She would be allowed to savor his company for the next several hours. She had her interfering aunt to thank for that. Willa glanced down at the front of her mother's good rose silk. Ruined. If only she were not spattered with mud and rotten fruit.

Lady Alameda stepped into her carriage, and the coachman shut the black lacquered door behind her.

"Well?"

Before answering her traveling companion's question, Honore settled herself on the velvet squabs and tapped her umbrella against the ceiling. The coach lurched forward.

Mattie asked again, "What did ye think of her?"

Honore laughed and clapped her hands together. "Priceless. She's priceless. Oh, Mattie, what fun we will have. She already has an attachment. Young Alex Braeburn, I can't remember what I heard about him. It will come to me. An interesting fellow, who may prove to be just as diverting as my antiquated niece."

Mattie's tongue clucked as she shook her head. "Don't tell me ye're up to yer games again? Honore, sweeting, remember last Season, an' poor Fiona. I doubt the child has yet recovered from what ye put her through. Ye must promise not to carry things too far this time."

"Bah, don't make such a fuss. I only carry things as far as they need to go. Anyway, last I heard, Fiona was rusticating in the country, great with child. No doubt Wesmont hovers over her like wet nurse. All very tedious, if you ask me.

"On the other hand, our little Wilhemina hasn't a tedious bone in her body. This should prove a very amusing arrangement."

"Amusing? Ye *are* at yer games. Here I thought ye wanted a young lady to train and mold into the daughter you never had, someone to love you when I am dead an' gone. I'm getting old, Honore. Ken ye not see the gray hairs in me old head?"

Honore's knee bobbed restlessly up and down. She drew in a loud breath and exhaled. "Stop badgering me, Mattie. I'll do as I please."

"Aye. That's what worries me."

Willa sat next to Alex on the small seat of the dog-cart. There was so little room on the seat that Willa's shoulder and thigh came in frequent contact with his. Each time she brushed against him and felt the hardness of his muscles, she grew more tense. She felt like leaping from the cart and running away as fast as she could. She also felt like throwing her arms around Alex's neck and kissing him violently.

Both actions were, of course, unacceptable. Instead, she prayed that he could not smell the fermented fruit on her dress as readily as she could.

"I must smell ghastly." She tried to sound sophisticated. When that failed, she experimented with a giggle. She was unaccustomed to giggling. It sounded false, flat, and silly. She was not the silly sort. She made a mental note not to attempt it again.

Alex leaned toward her and sniffed her shoulder. He wrinkled his nose and sat back. "Yes, Miss Linnet, I believe you have gone off. You will have to feed that dress to the chickens."

He smiled, but Willa didn't feel like smiling back. She was sitting next to, quite possibly, the most dashing man she could ever hope to meet. And he thought she smelled like something that should be thrown to the chickens. She adjusted her glasses and glared at the road ahead. His shoulders quivered. The cad was laughing at her.

"I see I've offended you. What a great simpleton I am. Pardon my manners. I should have said that you smell like a fine wine, ripening with age."

Willa tilted her nose even farther into the air and ignored him.

Alex laughed out loud. Euripides stopped stiff in his tracks, lifted his tail, and emitted a noisy puff of gas before walking on. Alex flicked the traces. "At least, you smell considerably better than that."

"How kind you are." Willa crossed her arms vehemently across her bosom. "You must stop flattering me, Mr. Braeburn, before I swoon."

"I seriously doubt you're the swooning type."

"You're probably right. I seem to be lacking in all of the maidenly arts."

Alex cast a sidelong glance at Willa's shapely torso. Memories of her innocent kisses warmed his blood. "Oh, I wouldn't say that."

Willa blushed.

He grinned.

She decided to introduce a new subject, one less personal. "My aunt is an unusual woman, is she not?"

"Unusual? Yes. Although, I don't think 'unusual' adequately describes her. I might have chosen a word like 'overbearing.'"

"I apologize for her behavior. She ought not to have ordered you about as she did."

"One must make allowances. After all, I did meet the lady whilst her niece was slung over my shoulder. It's quite possible, we got off to a wrong start."

"Yes, I suppose. However, I have it on good authority that Aunt Honore is mad as a hatter."

"London is full of eccentric ladies. It's the goal of many older women to be esteemed an 'original.' I believe your aunt more than qualifies for that epigram."

"If older ladies wish to be viewed as originals, why is it drummed into the head of every young woman that she must behave in an unoriginal manner? Indeed, it is high praise to be esteemed 'unexceptional.' A commendation I have yet to earn."

"You are assuming the *haute ton* is rational. Let me assure you, London society is anything but sensible."

"You seem sensible enough."

"Ah, but just yesterday you decided I was a rake, a gambler, and a scapegrace. Hardly a pattern card for sensibility."

She stared at him for a minute, unable to find a rcady answer. True, she'd ascribed each of those attributes to him. He probably deserved each characteristic. Yet she felt small for having said so. He was also witty and likable. He had rescued her from the fruit throwers, and now he was driving her home to prevent Aunt Honore from giving Euripides away. Further to the point, Euripides was actually clipping along instead of dawdling like a tortoise.

"How did you get Euripides to trot? He never trots."

Alex laughed. "I'd like to say it's my irresistible charm. I could pretend it's my superior horsemanship. But I suspect old Euripides is showing off for my mare."

As if on cue, the mare tied behind the cart whickered. Euripides's ears perked up, and he tossed his head to the side. It looked as though he were trying to catch a glimpse of Alex's horse.

"See what I mean?"

"It's absurd, but yes, my foolish mule is flirting with your mare."

"Absurd? Foolish? Since Adam met Eve, males have been doing things they wouldn't otherwise do, just so they can stare at a pretty face."

Alex flashed his one-sided, dimpled grin at her, and Willa's breath caught in her throat. She fought to keep the heat from rising in her cheeks. *Do not act like a silly schoolgirl.*

She shifted uncomfortably, searching for a suitable rejoinder. Her eyes lit on his horse trotting behind them. The large chestnut mare had a handsome white blaze down her slender nose. It contrasted nicely with her dark red color.

Willa cleared her throat. "To Euripides's credit, your mare is very pretty."

"Thank you." Alex grinned mischievously. "I think so, too. I admire red hair on females."

That was too much. Her cheeks grew unbearably hot. She knew she looked like a blushing idiot. Willa clasped her hands together and plunked them into her lap. "You are truly insufferable."

"Insufferable, I? You wound me. I merely meant to compliment you."

"Ha! You were toying with me. You know as well as I that red hair is considered disagreeable. You must think it great sport to make me blush. Well, don't gloat overmuch, Mr. Braeburn—"

"Alex."

"Mr. Braeburn. I turn red easily. After all, I'm just a provincial, not one of your sophisticated London ladies, of which I'm sure you have many. I rarely hear such blatant flattery. And when I do, it is always directed at my intelligent conversation. Never my appearance. I cannot be responsible for my foolish blushes. Let me assure you, my mind is not as easily gulled as my cheeks are."

"Hmm. Do you mean to tell me, your mind does not influence that scarlet color climbing higher on your cheeks?" He studied her with mock seriousness.

She shook her head and repressed, with difficulty, the urge to laugh.

He turned his attention back to the reins. "If you expect me to apologize you'll be waiting till doomsday. We insufferable barbarians compliment anyone we please."

Willa clapped her hands over her face. The man was outside of enough. A barbarian making compliments, indeed. Her nervousness and embarrassment, combined with his flummery and ludicrous arguments, created a bubbling stew inside her. Her shoulders started to shake. When they did, she erupted in laughter.

Suddenly, it didn't matter to Willa that she stunk to high heaven. She relaxed. The sunshine gently warmed her, the grass and flowers glowed vividly, and the sky was a magnificent gold-tinged blue. St. Cleve looked like the most inviting village in all of Britain. For a few brief moments, all was right with the world.

Then, the dogcart rolled to a stop in front of the vicarage and Willa's heart sank. Now, it would all end.

Alex would dine with them. Afterward, he would

wave farewell, and return to London, back into the arms of his exotic paramours. Visions of veiled women with almond-shaped eyes danced in her head.

She must collect her straying wits.

4

Little Bo Peep Has Lost Her Sense

Aggie stomped into Willa's bedchamber. "I can't abide that woman!"

Willa squeezed her wet hair over a copper basin and looked up. "Aunt Honore?"

"No. Well, I don't like her much neither. But I'm meaning that great hulking Scotswoman, Mattie. I'm going to run her through with a carving knife if she don't get out of my kitchen. She's the bossiest creature I ever did see. '*My mistress don't like cabbage. My mistress can't eat shellfish. Here, let me show ye how to fix them quail.*' I'll run her through, that's what I'll do."

"*Those* quail." Willa wrapped a towel around her hair. "Do try to get along, Aggie. It's just for one evening. I'm sure Aunt Honore plans to leave first thing in the morning."

Aggie folded her arms across her chest and tapped her toe. "At least, give me permission to throw her maid out of my kitchen."

"I don't know, Aggie. Perhaps the woman might teach you how to make some of those fancy dishes they serve in London."

"Humph. Nothing wrong with good Suffolk cooking," Aggie muttered under her breath. "That Scottish cow isn't going to teach me anything."

Willa plopped down on the bed and looked forlornly at the wardrobe doors. "I wish I had something beautiful to wear tonight."

"Your closet is full of lovely gowns."

"Yes, but twenty years out of fashion. You should have seen all the fine-looking ladies today. Their dresses were so unencumbered and elegant."

"You mean French-like and indecent. Londoners is wicked folk, and you would do well to remember it, miss."

"Londoners *are* wicked," Willa corrected softly, but Aggie had already marched out of the room. Willa sat alone on the bed, trying to figure out what she would wear to dinner. Which dress would *he* like the best? It shouldn't matter. He would leave and she would never see him again. What did it matter what she wore. But she did care. No sense lying to oneself. She still remembered the feel of his lips, his hands on her waist. Suddenly, she knew which dress.

When she finally approached the stairway leading to the parlor, it was with great trepidation. She had coiled her wet hair onto her head and donned her mother's blue silk. It had a very narrow waist, which Willa could barely squeeze into. She had tightened her corset so much that she could only breathe from the top of her lungs. Unfortunately, the wide collar flattened her breasts so severely they oozed up like bread dough. She covered them by draping a lace shawl around her neck, and tucking it into the collar. The gown was too short for modern standards, but it couldn't be helped. Willa gulped a quick shallow breath before starting down the steep dark staircase.

* * *

Alex sat in uncomfortable silence across from his brother and Jerome in the vicarage parlor. His chair was a small wooden-backed affair with very little padding and worn tapestry covering the seat. His companions had taken up positions in two ancient leather chairs near the fireplace, obviously a very familiar arrangement. The brass clock on the writing desk ticked loudly. Alex was cursing, for the fourteenth time, the dementia that had possessed him to accept such an invitation, when the stairs creaked.

They all looked up. Willa's slippered feet slowly descended the steps, followed by her naked ankles, and then far too much of her legs. Finally, her full skirts rustled into view. Alex watched attentively as Willa revealed more of her unusual costume with each step, her cinched-in waist, the flattened bodice, and the bust ineffectively covered by an old lace neckcloth. When her magnified blue eyes came into view, he felt her nervousness. Something caught in his throat. He coughed, but it didn't go away.

The men shuffled to their feet. Alex noticed that Daniel avoided making eye contact with Willa as he mumbled an awkward greeting. Jerome said nothing. His nose lifted perceptibly, as if a bad stench had just floated into the room. They lapsed into strained silence.

Alex bowed with far more formality than the occasion required. "A delight, Miss Linnet. I thought you would never return to us. But what is this? No more fruit? Not even a morsel left for us hungry souls?"

She smiled at him. There it was. Her gift of genuine warmth. Too bad more women couldn't smile with such a lack of artifice.

"Good evening, gentlemen." Lady Alameda stood in the doorway.

Alex stepped back, his eyelids lowered as he watched the countess make her theatrical entrance into the ramshackle little vicarage parlor. She swished toward Jerome, wearing a gown fit for the Prince Regent's drawing room, deep purple with shimmering beadwork. She dangled a plum-colored fan, and matching feathers paraded out of a comb in her hair. Jerome and Daniel gaped like yokels as she walked up to her nephew and planted a kiss on each cheek.

The stunned vicar finally pulled his jaw back up to where it belonged and stammered an introduction of the illustrious lady to his friend. Daniel bowed regally.

Alex coughed—this time to choke back a guffaw at his brother's overdone obeisance.

Honore turned in his direction. "Ah, Mr. Braeburn." She emphasized the *mister,* her eyes flashing with challenge.

Alex acknowledged her by inclining his head in a marginally acceptable greeting. The countess reminded him of something, what was it? Perhaps, a wily mongoose he had seen on his trip to India, or more likely, a dancing cobra.

She turned her attention to Willa. "Egad, child! What a fascinating dress. Are you in costume? You should have warned me, I have a delightful Egyptian ensemble I could have sent for. But no, my dear, I see by your face it is not a costume."

"It belonged to my mother."

"And her mother before her, no doubt. Have you nothing from this century?"

Willa's chin shot in the air. "No sense spending money on frivolities."

Alex silently applauded her refusal to be cowed. Although, it was an unusual sentiment, coming from a female. She couldn't mean it. Women lived for such things, did they not? But then, Willa was different from any female he'd ever known.

"*Frivolities?* Good heavens!" Honore rounded on Jerome. "What nonsense have you been pouring into this child's ear? Are you so clutch-fisted that you won't even purchase a new gown for your sister?"

Jerome tried in vain to loosen his collar as he faced the inquisition. His voice wobbled like that of a teenage boy. "It's a perfectly good dress."

"Piffle!" The countess waved her hand through the air. "Are you blind, man? Can you not see the girl's bosom is bursting out of this bodice? If she can breathe at all, it's a wonder."

Alex could not restrain himself from reinspecting the bosom in question. Yes. *Bursting*. True. Lovely, he thought. Quite lovely. Willa self-consciously tried to adjust her lace, to no avail. With some difficulty, he forced himself to stop looking.

Honore gave Willa's skirt a twitch. "Look at this. If it showed any more of her legs she would be arrested. Really, Jerome, perfectly good, indeed! Perfectly indecent!"

Honore held out the skirt, providing a more complete vista of Willa's legs as she continued her tirade. Jerome and Daniel turned their heads politely away, Jerome to the floor and Daniel to the clock. Alex took one look at Willa's face and knew she was mortified.

Enough. He squared his shoulders. "My lady, if you will kindly let go of her gown, a little less of Miss Linnet will be exposed. In so doing, you might spare the good vicar and my brother a heart seizure."

Lady Alameda flung down the blue silk. "Well, they

ought to be embarrassed. It's appalling to see the gel in a gown that dates back to the fall of Rome."

The vicar sputtered. "Rome? But, surely . . ."

Alex watched Willa's face as she battled with her emotions. She turned to her aunt, lifted her index finger in what he knew must be a prelude to a lecture. She opened her mouth, but stopped and regrouped. Anger, or perhaps frustration, galloped across her delightfully candid features. Alex guessed she was trying to compose a scathing set-down for the insensitive Lady Alameda.

Mercifully, Jerome's sour-faced housekeeper interrupted the impending battle. "Dinner is served, or it will be, if you would all like to retard to the dining room."

Willa groaned. "*Retire.* Retire to the dining room."

"That's what I said." Aggie imperiously left the parlor.

5

Pease Porridge Hot

Pease soup. Willa sent a silent prayer to heaven, begging that the rest of the dinner would not be so meager. She should have advised Aggie about the menu. Alex would think they were paupers, or worse, laughably provincial. She didn't think she could bear any more humiliation today.

Honore sniffed her spoon, as if the concoction were something the mule had dropped. "Pea soup, how charming. I haven't eaten pea soup in nearly a decade."

Willa shot her aunt a quelling glance, not that the woman could be quelled. Indeed, it would take an act of parliament and several strong soldiers to put a stop to her insults. "Try it, my lady. It's quite tasty. In any case, you cannot expect to find London delicacies here in St. Cleve. We are simple country folk."

Honore laughed. "Simple, my dear? I doubt it. You seem to be anything but simple. Refreshing, let us say you are refreshing country folk."

Aggie pushed through the side door, bearing the first course, under a tray full of covers. Willa held her breath as Aggie revealed each dish and set it on the table *en famille* style, mackerel with gooseberries, roast quail, boiled potatoes, artichokes with bean sauce, parsnips, and apple pudding. Dinner would not be the disaster Willa had feared.

She smiled with relief at Aggie. Aggie acknowledged her with a smug look as she left the room.

Willa cut a small piece of fish and skewered it onto her fork along with a sliver of potato and a small parsnip. As she slipped this composition into her mouth, she noticed Alex looking at her. Her cheeks flushed hot, and she was grateful for the dim light. Nevertheless, the fish seemed to swell in her mouth. It all went down her throat in a great lump. She looked across the table and noticed that her aunt, too, was studying her. Willa grabbed her wineglass and gulped the contents down. It would take more than that to steady her nerves.

Honore turned to Jerome. "Are you not curious, Jerome, what has precipitated my visit?"

His mouth full of victuals, Jerome nodded. "Yes, yes, indeed I am, Aunt. Naturally, we're honored that you would pay us a visit. I had in my mind to inquire if you had any particular purpose in it. I believe the last time we saw you Willa was still wearing short skirts."

"Still in them it appears."

Jerome tut-tutted, muttering under his breath. "Dress is perfectly fine."

Honore tapped her glass. "Very well, I will tell you why I've come. I bring you glad tidings—good news for all of us." She paused until everyone's attention rested on her.

Glad tidings, indeed. Her aunt sounded rather like a bawdy annunciation angel, ruminated Willa, stuffing a bite of herbed quail into her mouth.

"I've come to take Wilhemina to live in London with me."

Willa nearly choked.

Honore glanced around the table. "Why are you all staring at me as if I just sprouted horns? I am offering to make Willa my protégée, to introduce her to polite society. This is an extremely generous offer."

Willa took a quick look at Alex. Impossible to know what he was thinking, his lips were pursed and eyes narrowed.

Jerome recovered from his shock, and after what appeared to be a few simple calculations, his undisguised enthusiasm overflowed. "Extremely generous. Do you mean to pay for Willa's comeout?"

Honore nodded.

Alex frowned. Willa thought she heard him mutter, "Not a good idea."

Sir Daniel poked Jerome in the arm with the butt of his fork. "Think of it, my friend. Willa might go to London for the Season, meet an eligible *partí,* and all of our problems will be solved."

Alex's frown deepened.

Her brother's face lit up. "Yes, yes. It might answer. Willa has a dowry. It's small, but not insignificant. Surely some fellow in London—"

"You misunderstand me, gentlemen," Honore interrupted. "I have no intention of puffing Willa off. Of what use would she be to me married? I mean to make her my protégée, a companion."

"Ah." Alex straightened, his eyebrows arched as if he'd finally solved a vexing riddle. "There it is. The rub."

The fish turned to lead in Willa's stomach. He was right. Companion. Hardly an introduction into society. Scarcely a life at all.

Honore glared at him. "A surrogate daughter, of sorts. I have no children of my own. She has no parents. What could be simpler?"

"Calculus. Plato." Alex twirled his knife as if it were the most fascinating instrument he'd ever laid eyes on.

Jerome beamed at Honore. "This is an extremely generous offer. We will be delighted—"

"No." Willa shook her head. "We *would* be delighted, but unfortunately it is out of the question."

All eyes turned toward her.

She ignored them. She'd given her answer. There was nothing more to discuss. "Ah, here's Aggie with our dessert. Raspberry tarts, my favorite."

Aggie stood in the doorway, listening to their conversation with a stricken look on her face. She nodded at Willa and laid the tarts out on the table.

"Why?" Honore demanded. "Why is it out of the question?"

Aggie scowled.

Alex glanced expectantly at Willa.

She calmly set down her fork, and attempted to tap the tips of her fingers together, just as Daniel and Jerome usually did before launching into a lecture. Unfortunately, she missed. So, she clasped them together and tried not to look as if she were pleading. "Surely, it must be apparent. Jerome needs me here at the vicarage."

Jerome shook his head. "Oh no, Willa. I can manage just fine without—"

Willa grabbed the edge of the table. "What about the needy parishioners? Who'll take the sick baskets and mend clothing for the poor?"

"Plenty of women to do that sort of thing."

"Plenty," echoed Sir Daniel, nodding as he prepared for his next bite of tart.

Willa looked from one to the other, completely astonished. "You both act as if I wouldn't be missed at all."

"Of course we'll miss you." Jerome adjusted his dessert plate and readied his fork.

"Certainly, we'll miss you." Sir Daniel smiled with forbearance, as one does to a small child who has just been given a piece of hard candy, a pat on the head, and told to run along and play. "No one reads Greek poetry with as much feeling as you do."

Willa shot Sir Daniel a fiery glare in return for his paltry commemoration.

Honore's tone sounded silky and purring. "You see, my dear? There is nothing standing in your way."

"Except common sense." Alex cracked the shell on his tart. The juice ran out, drowning the pale helpless crust in deep dark red.

Honore smiled at him most peculiarly.

Willa shoved a forkful of raspberries into her mouth and wondered if she'd eaten a bad mushroom and slipped into lunacy. Or perhaps she was asleep and this was merely a serpentine concoction of her unconscious mind. If she pinched herself, it was quite possible she would wake up and the last two days will have been nothing more than a dream. She glanced at Alex. A dream containing some unforgettable fantasies. And a great deal of madness.

Alex deplored the thought of the supercilious countess taking Willa to London and corrupting her. Willa was like a mountain stream, pure and uncontaminated. He dreaded what London would do to her. It was like putting a prize mare to pulling a dray—a shameful waste.

Alex cleared his throat. "It seems obvious Willa doesn't want to go to London."

Lady Alameda's spine stiffened, and she glared in his direction. "That's ridiculous. What young lady, in her right mind, wouldn't want to go to London? And what *place* would you consign her to, Mr. Braeburn? This rustic little village? I think you do not see her potential."

He set his spoon down with rather more force than he'd anticipated. "Potential has nothing to do with it. London is full of undesirable elements. She has no experience with such things."

"Spoken like a gentleman who has been amongst the wrong kind of company." The countess trumped him neatly.

He pressed his lips tightly together, holding himself in check.

The lady with the whiplash tongue pushed her dessert plate away and snapped open her fan. "Aside from that, I cannot see how you have anything to say in the matter."

"True enough," confirmed Jerome. "I think it will be a splendid opportunity for my sister."

Alex flexed his jaw muscles. They were right. He had no say in it. He picked up his fork and stabbed the bleeding tart. None of his affair. Why should he trouble himself? He glanced at Willa. Because, never in his life had he met such a complete innocent.

She leaned toward her brother and made a gentle appeal. "No, Jerome, Alex is right. I don't want to go. I don't belong in London. Can't you see how out of place I would be in Aunt Honore's circles?"

"Nonsense, child." Honore stood up. "Come. Let us leave the gentlemen to their port."

As Alex watched Willa reluctantly follow her aunt

out of the room, he knew that the matter was settled. Lady Alameda would have her way. What chance did she stand against a woman like that? No, the enchanting little Willa would go to London and become yet another insipid, vacuous female. A shame. He swallowed Jerome's weak brandy in one gulp and set his glass down for a refill.

"I'm not going." Willa flopped down on the parlor settee.

"No?"

"Absolutely not."

"Hmm. Interestingly enough, I had thought you had a fairly good reason to go."

Willa frowned at Honore as if she were daft. "What do you mean? I stated my objections clearly. Every point I mentioned supported the argument for staying here, in St. Cleve."

"Piffle. I hear a little girl making noises like a frightened mouse. Afraid of London. Afraid of the *haute ton*. Do you plan on cowering here amongst these bumpkins for the rest of your life?"

"I'm not cowering." Willa caught her bottom lip between her teeth. True, she had wished for a more exciting life, daydreamed of it incessantly. Here was her opportunity, and yet she was refusing to go. Why. Maybe she was cowering.

"I think you are. You have a most compelling motive to come with me to London and yet—"

"What motive? What reason? I told you before—"

"The tall muscular motive, with the intriguing brown eyes. The Corinthian in your dining room with curly hair and a melting disposition whenever he looks in your direction."

"Alex? That's absurd."

Honore inspected her fingernails and waited.

Willa pressed a hand over her heart and stopped breathing like a rabbit. "I'm not the kind of woman he . . . He doesn't . . . I mean, he would never—"

"Oh, yes, he does. And yes, he would. The question is, my dear, do you? Would you?"

Horrid hot flames engulfed Willa's cheeks. Drat! She had unquestionably turned scarlet. She sat helplessly exposed to her aunt.

"Ha. As I thought. And do you expect this *Alex* to hang about the countryside rusticating? No. Let me assure you, come daylight that young man will be headed back to Town, and in a week or two he'll have forgotten you ever existed."

Willa stared at her hands folded neatly in her lap and tried to keep her breathing even and temperate. What could she do? Alex was a man of the world, completely unsuitable, and aside from that, he was far beyond her touch.

"As you say, Alex is a Corinthian. I have no expectations in that quarter."

"Not with *that* namby-pamby attitude." Honore took her fists from her hips and leaned toward Willa, using her fingers to describe a thin thread. "No, your Alex is a large trout caught on a very slender line. One must reel him in slowly, cautiously. Naturally, he'll thrash about from side to side. But, oh my! What a merry chase it will be." Honore stepped back. One side of her mouth curled up. "But, it may be you're not up to the challenge."

"I'm not a half-wit. I can see you're daring me. I'm not so gullible as you think. And how disrespectfully you speak of him—a trout on a line, indeed. Alex is a man, not a fish."

"Oh? So, you're not interested."

"I didn't say that. My foolish emotions are probably obvious to everyone. But, don't mistake the matter. I am, as in all things, ruled by my intellect, not my heart. Aside from that, I would *never* set out to catch a man as if he were a witless fish. Never."

"Very well, stay here in St. Nowhere. I'll choose another niece to adopt as my protégée. Let Alex spend the rest of his days wondering aimlessly, a rascal with no purpose. Who cares?" Honore rose and shook out her skirts.

Willa remained seated and studied her hands, which were clenched into a tight ball on her lap. Honore was right. In London she might cross paths with him occasionally—it would be better than never seeing him again. It was now or never. St. Cleve for the rest of her life, or take a chance on something different.

"Wait," she said softly and stood up.

Honore whipped around like a great purple-beaded hawk, narrowing her eyes at her niece.

"I'll go. On the condition that you must promise not to think of Alex as a fish." The eager glint in her aunt's eyes made Willa hesitate. "Nor a fox you intend to run aground with a pack of hounds. He is quite beyond my aspirations." When her aunt appeared willing to comply, she continued. "The truth is, I would like to come with you so that I may see a bit of the world before I return to spend the rest of my days here, in service to my brother and the people of my village."

Honore put her arm around Willa's shoulder and patted her.

"Whatever you say, *ma chère.* We shall deal with young Braeburn as if he were, not a fish, or a fox, but a noble lion on the African plain." With her free hand she described the broad flat vista of the African plains. Willa grimaced at her headstrong aunt.

"No?" Honore burst out laughing. "Come, let's tell the gentlemen our happy news."

They entered the dining room arm in arm. Willa stared at the floor while Honore tugged her forward.

"It is all decided. Wilhemina goes to London with me in the morning."

Willa glanced up in search of Alex's face. He was staring into his glass of brandy. He lifted the snifter in mock salute to her and tossed the contents down his throat.

The dining room door squeaked and clicked shut. Willa surmised that Aggie had been listening at the door. To confirm her suspicions, a great wail vibrated from the kitchen. Good grief, the woman was bawling like a cow in need of milking.

Aggie suddenly ceased crying and began bellowing. "Get out of my kitchen, you great Scottish witch! Out! Out!"

The sound of crockery smashing against the wall sent Willa running into the kitchen. It took several minutes, and several drastic promises, to calm Aggie down.

When Willa returned to the dining room, Sir Daniel and Alex were gone. Her heart sank. What was she doing, haring off to London with a madwoman? Leaving the home and the people she loved. In that single moment, the disappointment she'd witnessed in Alex's face played back to her a hundred times. Her corset suddenly seemed to tighten painfully against her lungs.

6

She Put Her in a Pumpkin Shell

Two days later, their carriage clattered to a stop in front of Lady Alameda's London town house, Alison Hall. Lady Alameda, her maid Mattie, Willa, and a very haggard Aggie filed out of the coach. Aggie straggled up the stairs behind them.

Honore clasped Willa's elbow and guided her into the house. "Why you insisted on bringing that wretched woman with you, I cannot understand. She did nothing but get sick and make all of us miserable."

"Poor Aggie. I don't think she's ever ridden so far in a coach before. She's lived all of her life in St. Cleve."

"She would've done well to stay there."

"I don't think she could have borne it. She's been with me since I was born."

Honore snorted. "Just keep her out of my way."

Aggie stumbled through the front doors and gasped. She and Willa stared open-mouthed at Honore's marble entry hall. Four huge Doric columns vaulted three stories to a domed glass ceiling. The Grecian motif was carried into the circular marble staircase. The walls were set with white relief sculptures of Greek gods. Willa adjusted her glasses in an attempt to see more details.

"Aunt Honore, this is magnificent, truly magnificent. I never would have guessed from the outside what marvels lay inside. Oh, look, Aggie! There is Orpheus, and over there are the nine muses. Isn't it wonderful?"

Aggie's mouth remained open.

Honore sniffed at the maid and looped her arm through Willa's. "Come. I want to show you to your rooms."

The neoclassic architecture fascinated Willa. The house was so open and spacious that it reverberated with light. It was better than any palace Willa had ever imagined. The rooms Honore led her to were larger than the entire first floor of the vicarage. Willa caught her breath.

"These can't be for me."

"Yes, my dear, they are." Honore signaled to her butler. "Cairn, send for Madame Brigitte. Tell her to come this afternoon and bring an army of seamstresses."

"Yes, m'lady." The tall white-haired servant bowed very precisely and looked down his long nose at Willa as he walked away. Willa felt as if she were a cuckoo in a nest of peacocks. She fiddled with the skirt of her worn traveling dress. "I'm afraid you can't make a silk purse out of a sow's ear, Aunt."

"Is that another of Jerome's favorite proverbs? You may rest easy, dearest. I have no intention of remodeling a pig's ear." She pinched at the fabric of Willa's sleeve. "I simply wish to provide a suitable wardrobe for my niece."

Honore rubbed her palms together as if eager for

the project to begin, and adopted a more instructive tone. "Now, you must not allow yourself to be intimidated by Madame Brigitte. Her real name is Ada Bainbridge, but it wouldn't do to call her that. She uses a French persona, because the ladies of the *ton* think only a French modiste will do. Nevertheless, the woman is a genius. You will see."

And see, she did.

That afternoon Madame Brigitte arrived, followed by troops of seamstresses carrying bolt after bolt of gorgeous fabrics.

"Green, I zink with ze red hair. Unless, m'lady, you wish ze débutante white? No, of course not. What was I thinking? Not good for my lady's protégée."

Willa stood with her arms extended while swatches of every color were draped over her and evaluated.

"Also, I have ze blue magnifique—take a look at ziz. With her eyes, it will be divine, yes?"

"Hhmm." Aunt Honore tapped her fingers against her cheek shrewdly scrutinizing each fabric. "Yes."

Madame Brigitte approached Honore with some temerity. "Perhaps, one white gown, yes? Against her red hair, it will show so nicely. I have ziz white Turkish taffeta, *extraordinaire.* See how it shimmers. White, but not debutante white, if you know what I mean."

Madame laid the iridescent cloth across Willa's shoulders. For hours, Willa was draped and measured and pinned and prodded and poked. Finally, Madame and her army marched away, and Willa threw herself down on a fainting couch.

Honore walked over to her and gently stroked Willa's wild curls. The next thing Willa knew, Honore was pulling a bell, summoning the very stiff butler into the room.

"Send for Monsieur Renellé. We must do something with this hair."

Willa groaned.

Five days later, after Willa had been coifed, properly outfitted with gloves, fans, slippers, and hats, after her face had been soaked in cucumber plasters, zinc creams applied to diminish her stubborn freckles, and after she had been manicured and perfumed, she decided to draw the line.

"Enough! I hardly recognize myself as it is. I will not give up my spectacles. I cannot see past my hand without them."

"Fiddlesticks! I'm not asking you to go without seeing. Just carry this lovely lorgnette instead of wearing those ugly wire things buckled to your nose. I myself carry a peering glass on many occasions. An elegant instrument, don't you agree?"

Willa refused to take it. She looked it over and shook her head.

"Why not?" Honore held up the ornate long-handled lorgnette to her eyes.

"I fail to see the advantage. It's merely a pair of spectacles on a gold stick. Remarkably inconvenient. I must hold it up every time I wish to see past my arm."

"Ah, but handled correctly, a peering glass can be as effective a social device as your fan."

"That's another thing. I can't possibly remember all those codes and signals connected with the fan. I'm certain I shall be suggesting an assignation with some poor fellow, when in truth, I am merely trying to cool my face."

"Oh bother, Willa! I know for a fact you are not as

thick as you pretend. We'll practice the fan business again this afternoon. Now take this glass and practice using it." Honore thrust the lorgnette into Willa's hand. "I must sort through my invitations and decide where we will go this evening. Perhaps we will attend Lady Haversburg's card party?"

"Cards? This evening? But I couldn't possibly. You see, my hands will be quite taken up, what with a fan dangling from this one, and the lorgnette in the other."

"Out!" Honore pointed toward the stairway. "Go pester that evil woman you inflicted on my household. Go!"

Willa tripped gaily up the stairs with a little smile on her face. She took unrepentant pleasure in her small victory. After all, Aunt Honore regularly harried her beyond endurance. She was so pleased with herself that she almost failed to notice Cairn quietly ushering a man wearing a dark coat into Honore's study below.

Honore leaned back in her chair and regarded her visitor. "Well? What did you learn?"

The man remained standing at attention and did not remove his long brown dustcoat. "Has rooms in Blackfriars Road, as you suspected he might. Goes out regular to Jackson's. Makes the rounds at Boodles, Watiers, and the Cocoa Tree. Been seen, frequently, in the company of a Mr. Erwin and Lord Tournsby. Both gents said to've had a run of bad luck of late. But, seems unlikely your fellow plays as deep as t'other two. No vowels lying about unpaid."

The visitor stopped speaking and stood stiffly with his hands clasped behind his back.

"And?"

"And what, m'lady?"

She tapped her fingernail against the varnished desktop. "Where does he go this evening?"

"Begging your pardon, m'lady, but I've no way of knowing." He shifted uneasily.

Honore kept her voice level and low, but the note of irritation could not be missed. "Well, find out."

"Could be, I won't know where he's going till I follow 'im to his destination."

"You're paid to find out. Bribe his valet. Do whatever you must, but find out."

"Gent doesn't employ a valet."

Honore rubbed her temple impatiently. "He has servants of *some* kind. Be creative. Perhaps, one of his friends. Tournsby, yes, that's it. The whole family has run dry. His pockets are to let. Try him."

Honore picked up her quill and began looking over a document. "Report back as soon as you know."

He pulled on his forelock and left as silently as he had come.

7

Mirror, Mirror on the Wall, Who's the Blindest of Us All

"She tricked me, Aggie. Now I'll have to use this ridiculous thing." Willa waved the lorgnette in the air. "I won't be able to see the stage without it."

Aggie clucked her tongue. "Now, Miss Willa, don't fuss. It's a lovely glass. See how the gold matches your dress. Much as I hate to admit it, your aunt has clever taste. You look as fine and elegant as any lady I ever seen."

"Saw."

Aggie nodded and clapped her hands together. "That's right. My little Willa is going to attend the Royal Opera House. I can't ne'er believe it."

Willa held the lorgnette up to her eyes and studied herself in the full-length oval mirror. White iridescent fabric draped gracefully over her figure, artfully designed so that it covered her while revealing her at the same time. Without her corset, she felt nearly naked, but Aunt Honore had insisted. A transparent overskirt, shot with gold threads, floated around the sides and back of her gown. With white flowers in her hair, she felt like a princess, albeit a half-naked princess.

"I'm an impostor."

"What can you mean?"

She turned away from the mirror. "It doesn't look like me."

"Don't be a goose. It's you, all right. You look 'xactly like the gentlewoman I raised you to be, that's what."

"Are you certain this neckline isn't too low? Without a corset my bosom looks horridly large."

Aggie sniffed, plucked at a thread on her old woolen skirt and shook her head. "I wouldn't say so, no. That dressmaker, what wasn't a frog after all, said as how all the best ladies wear low necklines."

Willa sighed and dangled the lorgnette from her wrist. "Let us hope you are right."

"You best be on your way now, sweeting. I'll be waiting up to hear all about it, so remember everything."

The white marble staircase seemed longer than Willa remembered. She tried not to stumble while walking down to meet her aunt and their escort. One of the tallest men she had ever seen stood next to her aunt. She raised the peering glass and looked up at him. Thin, well-dressed, with dazzling white hair, and a sharp beaklike nose, he gazed back at her with open curiosity.

Honore tugged on Willa's arm, forcing her to lower the lorgnette. "Where have you been? We have been waiting for nearly an age. Lord Monmouth, allow me to present my niece, Miss Wilhemina Linnet. Lord Monmouth has kindly agreed to escort us to Covent Garden for the evening."

He nodded politely. Willa dropped a curtsy. Escorted by this statuesque man, there would be no way to escape anyone's notice, probably the very reason Aunt Honore had chosen him to accompany them to the opera.

"Come along, dear. Monmouth's cattle are standing."

They piled into his carriage and drove slowly onto St. James's and then into heavy traffic on Hart Street. Honore grew impatient. "This crush is all because of those infernal elephants Kemble is putting on the stage. Everyone and his uncle must come to see them."

"Real elephants?" Willa could not believe it. "On stage?"

Honore flicked her hand, as if it were a trifle. "During the pantomime, I expect."

Monmouth rested his cane against the squabs. "I rather think this heavy traffic is owing to Mrs. Siddons's performance. It's rumored she'll not remain on the stage much longer."

Willa could not fathom her good fortune, elephants and Mrs. Siddons all in one night. "I've heard her portrayal of Lady Macbeth is the best of all time."

"You may judge for yourself tonight." Honore snapped open her fan and stirred a small breeze. "If her brother Kemble would stop turning the stage into a circus so often she might stay on it a few years more."

"Whatever the cause," Lord Monmouth said with equanimity. "London shall feel the loss keenly when she retires."

The coach rolled to a halt on Bow Street, where its occupants disembarked and entered the portico of the Royal Opera House. They climbed the stairway to the saloon behind the private boxes. Willa marveled at the enormous Greek statuary adorning the walls. She was so absorbed in the architecture she scarcely noticed the other patrons staring at her.

Honore whispered in Monmouth's ear. He leaned down to Willa, who was on his other arm. "Lady Alameda would like you to stop staring at the walls as if they were more interesting than the people. I believe she wishes to convey to you that one's purpose in attending the opera house is to see and be seen." Willa listened carefully as Monmouth continued to whisper instructions.

It was in this moment of innocent intimacy that Alex, standing across the room, caught sight of her. His breath snagged in his throat.

It was her. Willa. An incredible Willa. A small, voluptuous goddess. The marble statues were pale imitations next to her warmth and vitality. Her red hair glittered with golden sparks. Her enticing, diminutive figure aroused his senses. He wanted to scoop her up and carry her away.

Damn their eyes! Every man in the room was leering at her. He took a deep breath and drained his glass of woefully weak punch.

What had come over him that he should feel possessive? It was impossible. Women like Willa were made for marriage and family. Alex Braeburn had no interest in either one. Nevertheless, he heartily wished Monmouth would stop whispering in the girl's ear.

He would not stand here in the saloon and ogle her like a lovesick schoolboy. Ludicrous. She was merely the vicar's little sister. Nobody. A provincial. He pictured her in that preposterous Georgian shepherdess dress she'd worn at the vicarage. Instead of hardening his mind against her, it made him smile and shake his head. Ridiculous dress. He remembered all too well how the short skirt exposed her delicate white ankles and calves.

And here he was, drooling over her like a nodcock again. Alex thumped his tumbler onto a waiter's tray, and set off to find Lord Tournsby's box.

Willa felt someone staring at her. She lifted her lorgnette and focused, scanning the saloon. To her dismay, not one, but many people, stared at her. She swallowed hard, and hoped there was nothing vulgar or distasteful about her dress. The ladies' faces did not appear friendly at all. The gentlemen, on the other hand, made her uncomfortable with their flagrant inspection of her person. She was relieved when Honore urged them to take their places in the box.

The private boxes were Grecian pink and cream, with chairs upholstered in a light blue cloth. Willa felt transported into a fairy world. The patrons seated in their boxes were as dazzling as the surroundings. It looked as if hundreds of kings and queens had gathered for the evening's entertainment. From behind the crimson curtain, Mr. Kemble walked out onto the stage. The play was about to begin. Willa raised the lorgnette and leaned forward with all the eagerness of a child at Christmas. Not until the curtains closed for intermission did she take her eyes from the stage.

Lord Monmouth grinned at Willa. "I need not ask what you think of the play thus far, Miss Linnet. Pleasure is written upon your face." He chuckled. "Quite transfixed, was she not, Lady Alameda?"

"Exactly so. Transfixed. I cannot think of a better

word. Now, all of London must realize that this is her first visit to the theater."

"Come, my dear. No shame in having led a secluded life. Your niece is charming. Delightful company."

He smiled warmly at Willa, who lifted her peering glass to get a clearer view of his face.

He chuckled. "Charming. May I get you ladies some refreshment?"

Honore whispered in his ear. He nodded and left to retrieve their punch.

She turned to Willa. "My dear, you stayed glued to the stage like the veriest yokel."

"I'm sorry. The play was fascinating. I've read it so many times. Yet, to see it brought to life . . ." She searched for adequate words. "It was enthralling."

"Yes, well, try not to be so *enthralled* during the second half. Look around a bit, catch someone's eye and then carefully look away. Don't want anyone thinking I've taken a green girl under my wing."

"But? Is that not precisely what you've done?"

"Don't be ridiculous. Now then, any minute we're likely to have visitors. Do not gush about the play. But, don't sit there mute, either. Try to use that glass discriminately. Locate your quarry. Raise it and then lower it disinterestedly, for effect."

"I'm afraid, the effect may be that I will be seen addressing a column rather than one of our visitors."

"Folderol. You are being difficult again."

Before they could debate further, Lady Tricot and her daughter entered their box. The rotund woman had an abundance of heavy black hair coiled on her head and a sizable mustache of the same color. Her lavender silk gown and gauze overskirt bore disturbingly large stains where the lady perspired. In the close quarters of the box, the smell became almost overpowering. Aunt Honore whipped open her fan. Willa supposed that this did not signal anything other than a desire to move the air about.

Lady Tricot's daughter, Alfreda, was the antithesis of her mother. So willowy, Willa feared the girl might blow over in a breeze. Her astonishingly white hair was wispy and fine, making her appear almost ghost-like.

Willa tried to draw her into conversation but found it difficult to hear the girl's subtle replies. She leaned closer and caught tiny snatches of her visitor's lilting responses.

A noisy crowd gathered outside the doorway, blocked by Lady Tricot's ample frame.

"See here, Lady Alameda, how well your niece gets on with my Alfreda." Lady Tricot's voice echoed around the alcove and out into the theater. "Must bring the gel to m'breakfast alfresco next Thursday. Everyone there, eh? A little gathering for good friends, you know."

"Thank you, Margaret. We shall make every effort." Honore smiled tolerantly, but offered no further conversation.

After Lady Tricot pushed her way out of the box, it was as if a stone had fallen out of a dike. Callers flooded in, most of them gentlemen. Monmouth shoved through the crowd and handed Willa and Honore their glasses of punch.

He whispered cryptically to Honore, "Done."

Her aunt nodded and one corner of her mouth curled up.

They were up to something. Willa squinted, trying to bring her aunt's countenance into sharper focus. Exactly *what* was *done*?

She had little time to speculate. Monmouth stood at Willa's elbow and performed the introductions.

It was difficult for Willa to manage her punch cup and lorgnette at the same time. She let the eyeglasses dangle at her wrist, and smiled evenly at each new blurry face. Next time, she vowed, she would wear her spectacles no matter what her aunt said.

Alex fidgeted in the queue outside Lady Alameda's box. He overheard two matrons disparage Willa as they were leaving the box.

"Impertinent gel. Didn't even look at me when I was speaking to her."

"No?!" The other woman clucked her tongue. "And she frowned at me, just as if she were the Queen Mother herself. Still, she *is* Honore's niece. One can't simply ignore her."

"More's the pity."

Spiteful cats, thought Alex. He stopped short. There it was again, that protective feeling. This was a mistake. He shouldn't have told his friends he was acquainted with her. He ought to stay as far away as possible.

"Wearisome crush." Alex scowled at Lord Tournsby and Harry Erwin. "Why are we standing about just to meet a chit from the country?"

Tournsby grinned sardonically. "Alex, old fellow, have your wits gone begging? The *chit* has a prime figure and she's La Alameda's niece. Old girl has pots of money and no daughter of her own. Your delectable young acquaintance might be the remedy for my bothersome duns, and a palatable morsel into the bargain."

Harry nudged Alex good-naturedly in the ribs.

"Tournsby's right. Demmed fine-looking chit. Worth the wait, Braeburn."

Alex glanced at the ceiling and flexed his jaw. It was all he could do to keep from slapping the smirk off Tournsby's face.

"Didn't think *you* would stoop to fortune hunting."

"Such severe language, my friend." Tournsby brushed a fleck of lint from his lapel. "Time I set up my nursery. My father brought it to my attention just the other day, directly after he made a rather unfortunate excursion to White's." He laughed without the least hint of shame.

Alex muttered loud enough for his friend to hear. "I doubt there's enough money in the National Treasury to bail you, *and* your sire, out."

Tournsby shrugged. "Probably right. Still, every fellow seeks to improve his situation. Can't fault me for that. If one must marry, why not do it advantageously, eh?"

Alex exhaled loudly. "Because your taste runs toward a decidedly different sort of female, that's why. This one would bore you inside of three weeks."

"Perhaps, but her money wouldn't."

Harry tipped up on his toes to gander at Willa. "Don't know what you're on about, Braeburn. Take a look at her. Wouldn't bore me in the least."

Alex pressed a restrictive hand on Harry's shoulder, forcing the fellow back to ground. "Don't make a cake of yourself."

"But have you seen her? She's just my size." Harry held his hand level, measuring up to his nose. "Lovely height. Don't mind the red hair at all. Quite like it. A flame. Hope she has a personality to match."

Alex straightened his shoulders and looked down his nose at them. "Good grief! You've both gone daft.

She's a vicar's little sister. I had it directly from her brother, she only has a modest dowry."

Tournsby's eyes sharpened. "Oh ho, so you've checked into the matter. Well, perhaps the aunt has improved the situation. Monmouth hinted as much. We shall see. Look here, we have an opening and you promised us an introduction."

Alex swore under his breath and reluctantly followed Tournsby and Harry into Lady Alameda's box.

When he bowed beside Willa and softly called her name, she turned toward him like a whippet catching a scent.

"Alex?"

She couldn't see. He caught the dangling lorgnette on her wrist and tipped it up toward her face. She held the cumbersome opera glasses to her eyes, and he watched her lips form a smile. She didn't say anything. That smile perfectly communicated her rush of emotions.

He must have stared at her mouth too long. She surprised him by tugging on his sleeve. He leaned closer.

"Tell me the truth. No one else will. Is there something horribly amiss with this dress? I get the most awful stares from some of the other ladies. It's indecent isn't it?"

He examined her gown. The view afforded him from his height was primarily of her ample cleavage. He cleared his throat. What could he say? The dress is within the bounds of decency, but it shows your figure off to perfection. Your breasts are incredibly beautiful. Quite stunning. Naturally, the other women would like to have you thrown off a bridge. And the men want—he took a deep breath and shook his head. "Nothing. Nothing is amiss."

She exhaled. Relieved. He could see it. Just like everything she thought or felt, he could read it as plainly as writing on a page.

Tournsby dug his elbow sharply into Alex's ribs. "Forgotten the introductions, old man?"

Alex performed a halfhearted rendition of 'May I present,' and suffered through Tournsby's blatant flattery and leering. He noted, with pleasure, that after a fleeting glance at his incorrigible friend, Willa did not bother with the lorgnette.

Although, she obviously liked Erwin. When Harry bowed, the wretch came nearly face-to-face with her. She bestowed one of her genuine smiles on him. She *would* like Harry, the odd little turnip was like an overgrown puppy, bouncy and guileless. Just her type.

Alex turned sharp at Harry's last remarks. What in blazes was he saying?

"Must come! If you love horses. Simply the thing to do. Say you will? Braeburn's entering a horse. A real goer. Can't miss that, eh?"

Tournsby nodded sagely. "Yes. Just so. Mustn't miss the races." Remembering protocol with more alacrity than his zealous companion, Tournsby shifted his address to Lady Alameda. "What say you, my lady? A day at the races? Not the Derby, of course. Just a small affair out in Surrey."

Alex inhaled loudly and subtly shook his head, cueing Willa's aunt. She must decline. It wasn't right to put Willa in places where he must be privy to other men pursuing her. The least they could do is hold court somewhere miles away from him. Egypt perhaps. Or Antarctica.

The wicked woman grinned. "A wonderful suggestion. I adore the races. Yes, we'd be delighted."

Tournsby inclined his head. "My father's landau is quite spacious. We might all travel together quite comfortably, perhaps a small luncheon at an inn along the way?"

Honore's eyebrow lifted sardonically. "Your father still owns that rig? Thought he put it up for sale at Tattersall's. No matter. We would be pleased." She nodded and waved her fan, signaling an end to Tournsby's audience.

It was done then. Alex crossed his arms, annoyed at Lady Alameda and his scapegrace friend.

Tournsby lavished another self-ingratiating bow on the countess, just as if the rascal weren't wishing to tweak Lady Alameda's nose for her crack about auctioning off the landau. Tournsby excelled in pretense.

It didn't help Alex's mood any to note that Harry was still dribbling over Willa as though she were a Christmas pudding, stammering out overdone compliments, and laughing like a ten-year-old girl at everything she said.

Time to go. Alex hooked his pudgy friend's arm, nodded at Tournsby, and bowed to Willa. "I hope you enjoy your visit to London."

Willa blinked, straining to see him more clearly. He read the way she wished to hold him in the box longer. She desired more of his company. But she restrained herself. Willa wouldn't try to hold a man against his wishes. Not that she *could* hold him. No. That crestfallen expression in her eyes had absolutely no power to make him stay. He wished to go, and go he would. He couldn't bear to remain one more instant. He tried to move. Not another moment. "Until Sunday afternoon, then."

She smiled.

He thought for a moment the foot lamps on the stage had flared brighter. Perhaps, the play was about to begin again. He found a way to galvanize his feet. Good God, what was wrong with him?

"I'm in love," Harry gushed as they made their way out of the box and down the hallway.

"Don't be ridiculous." Alex gave his friend a thump.

8

Baa, Baa, Black Sheep, Have You Any Blunt?

Early the next morning, Alex rode out of Town. He wanted a breath of air that was not scented with Tournsby's plots or Harry Erwin's lovesick sighs.

He didn't have far to go before the fresh air cleared his head. Ah, the country, green fields and meandering hedgerows, where nothing was delineated in a straight line, land of contented disorder. He smiled at the lovely curling farmland.

It wasn't long before he turned down a less-traveled lane that led to a modest but well-kept estate. Squire Harley hailed him from the yard. Alex's horse's shoes clicked on the cobbled courtyard between the mews and the house. A stable boy ran to take Alex's mount.

The gentleman farmer was a large man, almost Alex's height, who greeted Alex with a hearty slap on the shoulder. "She's doing well, son. I expect she'll give birth any day now."

"Is she fit? Eating well?"

"Aye lad. Fit as a fiddle. Come and see for yourself. It'll do her a world of good to see you."

They headed for the stables. Alex found his one true love hanging her head over her stall door.

"There you are, my beauty. As lovely as the day we first met." She whickered and nodded, completely unabashed by his praise. He stroked her chestnut nose and patted her neck. "How are feeling, old girl? Let's have a look at you, shall we?"

He led the thoroughbred out of the stables and into the yard. She swayed under the huge burden of the foal she carried. Indeed, Alex thought, it jolly well better be born any day now. Darley's Lass couldn't bear much more weight without injury.

He pulled out a carrot he'd secreted in his pocket. As she contentedly crunched his offering, he gingerly checked her midsection.

"Her teats are waxing. She's overdue. Perhaps we should force the birth?"

The squire shook his head. "I don't recommend it. Often as not, that course turns out far worse than waiting. The farrier says she's healthy enough. She'll manage. Must be patient."

Alex nodded. "All the same, I don't want to lose her. She's given me four fine colts."

"Aye." He laughed. "I don't mind telling you, I've got a basket of eggs wagered on Mercury's Son."

Alex nodded. "Not too many eggs, I hope? It's his first race of any consequence."

"I've the advantage of having watched him exercise every morning. Never set eyes on a horse with as much wind in his sails as that one."

Alex stroked Darley's neck and tried without success to suppress his proud grin. "I've no doubt he'll make a good showing. It's his mother, here, I'm concerned about." Alex carefully checked her legs.

The squire clucked his tongue. "No need to fret. It'll be any day now. I'll send word as soon as she begins to foal."

"Or at the first sign of trouble. I'll keep you advised of my direction at all times." He clapped a hand on the squire's shoulder and faced him squarely. "I'm concerned about her, Harley. She's not just any broodmare. Darley's Lass is . . ." He frowned and looked away.

The squire nodded. "I know, lad. I understand."

Alex nodded, satisfied. "At the first inkling of change, send for me."

Later that afternoon, Alex rode away, considerably more relaxed than he'd been in several days. Not so relaxed, however, that he didn't mark the stranger at the end of the lane, a sturdy-looking fellow wearing a long coat, former soldier by the look of him. He lurked well back near the hedges until Alex turned onto the main road. When Alex glanced back, the stranger had headed up the lane leading to Harley's estate. Must be yet another discharged soldier wandering the countryside in search of work, Alex surmised, and dismissed his concern.

Alex approached his customary corner table at Boodles. Tournsby and Harry had their heads bowed together in earnest conference. A porter dressed primly in black silk knee breeches, standing at attention, gave a slight start as Tournsby slapped his hand loudly against the table.

"No, no. You cannot simply run her aground in her aunt's sitting room. Have a little more finesse than that, Harry."

Harry sniffed defensively. "I don't pretend to such things. Leave the finessing to you, I always say." He tipped up his glass of Madeira.

"Just as well." Tournsby sneered.

Alex signaled to the porter, and sat down with them. "What are you on about?"

Tournsby tapped one finger on the table. "Strategy, my friend. Strategy. A means to pulling myself out of the River Tick."

The porter set a scotch in front of Alex. "Plan to run off to America, do you?"

"Gad, no. Told you before. La Alameda's heir."

Before Alex could erupt, Harry interceded. "Too fine a chit for that sort of thing, Tournsby. I mean to beat you out. See if I don't."

Tournsby chuckled. "Small chance. Her aunt's bound to hang out for a title."

"Not when she finds you haven't a sou to your name." Harry sat up a little taller in his chair. "I, on the other hand, will be solvent come quarter-day."

Alex realized he was clenching his jaw. All the tension he'd sent sailing away this morning slammed back into his shoulders. "Turnips for brains, both of you. I told you before, she doesn't have but a modest dowry."

Tournsby shook his head. "Monmouth says different. The rumors are true. Spoke to the old fellow not more than two hours ago. Chit's bound to be the dowager's new heir. He had it from the lady herself."

"Which means naught. Consider Lady Alameda's history. For pity sake, Tournsby, she's as mercurial as our good king, but without his morality."

Harry plunked his glass down. "Don't matter. Most beautiful female I ever met. A pocket Venus. Don't care about her money."

Alex smiled patiently. "How very providential, considering there isn't any."

Tournsby twirled the amber liquid in his glass. One side of his mouth twisted up. "What's this, Alex? Trying to discourage the competition?"

Alex didn't bother responding. What difference did it make to him? None. None whatsoever. He raised his crystal tumbler. "By all means, gentlemen, strategize at will."

Tournsby glanced at him sideways, as if he wasn't convinced. Harry, on the other hand, nodded affably. "More like it. Could use your help, Alex. Don't want Neddie here making the gel's life a misery, do we?"

Tournsby chuckled dully. "That's the spirit. But listen carefully, Harry, don't call me by that ridiculous nickname in public again, or I'll break your knees." He paused long enough to make sure poor Harry grasped his meaning. "Now then, as I see it, we won't want to be viewed as suitors. Too common by half. I suggest we discover what events our young quarry plans to attend. We put in an appearance, as if it's merely a fortuitous coincidence. Then, contrive a way to get her alone. I believe a well-placed bribe might be in order. Alex, old chum, any blunt on you?"

Alex rested his head on his hand, kneading his forehead, and muttered, "With any luck she won't even see you."

Tournsby snorted. "Ha. You thought I didn't notice? I'm not completely dull-witted. Nearsighted, isn't she? Even better. An accident. We orchestrate an accident. With her poor vision, what could be simpler?"

Harry glared at Tournsby as the porter refilled his

Madeira. "Never say you plan to injure the gel? Wouldn't want to see her hurt. I'd have to call you out for such a thing."

Tournsby sighed with exasperation and answered flatly, hand over his heart. "Spare me, oh kind sir." Then he flicked Harry on the side of the head. "What do you take me for? I merely intend to set up a situation in which I might emerge a hero."

Harry smacked both hands on the table. "Sadly out there! Ought to be *me* cast as the hero. I'm the one what truly loves her."

"You're too short for the part. Aside from that, I'm the one with the plan." Tournsby leaned forward, warming to his scheme. "Lady Tricot is having an alfresco breakfast on the banks of the Thames. Boating accident. Might be just the thing." He tapped his finger speculatively.

Harry bristled up his shoulders. "I'll spike your guns, I will. I'll be the hero, or my name's not Harold Erwin."

Tournsby laughed. "Have at it, Harry. More fun all round if you do."

Alex leaned back in his chair, pressed his lips together, and rubbed his chin. The whole world had gone mad. Or perhaps this was one of those particularly annoying dreams following a night of too much drink and too little sleep. With any luck, he'd wake up and vomit the whole incident away. Either way, he'd had enough.

He stood up. "You've both got room to let in your brain-boxes. I wish you merry."

"Wait." Harry jumped up, nearly toppling his chair, and grabbed Alex's arm. "You've got to help me. Can't very well wage war against the likes of Tournsby without you."

Tournsby grinned. "By all means, Alex. Wouldn't want to miss a spectacle like this, would you? Will Harry save the chit? Or drown her in the process?"

Alex frowned.

Tournsby flicked his wrist and opened his palm, allowing the invisible answer to flutter away. "Besides, if the whole thing is an utter bore, you can pop over to see your horses. Not more than a few miles from Lady Tricot's estate to your stables."

"Out of the question." Alex folded his arms across his chest. "Not interested in watching the two of you make jackanapes out of yourselves."

"Suit yourself. Think of it though. Harry here, paddling around the Thames, trying to drag the vicar's little sister to safety. Entertaining thought, eh?"

"What ho? Could do for it." Harry straightened his waistcoat. "Don't doubt it for a minute."

Alex arched an eyebrow skeptically. "When was the last time you had a swim, Harry?"

"Dunno. Eton, I expect."

Tournsby hooted. "Splendid. I shall have to pull both of them out. Now, about that blunt for bribing the servants?"

Alex glanced up at the ornate ceiling. What he needed right now was divine help in suppressing a rather profane string of oaths he wanted to rain down on both their heads. Since he did not really expect heavenly assistance to be forthcoming, he turned and stalked out of the club, shutting his ears to Neddie's aggravating guffaws.

9

It Fell to Earth, I Know Not Where

Willa looked down at her slippered feet as she stood in the wet grass. These were not shoes for traipsing across a field, and yet here she was in the middle of Lady Tricot's huge lawn, wearing kid slippers.

The morning rain had dampened some of Lady Tricot's plans. Fortunately, the rain stopped at precisely eleven o'clock, in plenty of time for the breakfast, which began at two in the afternoon. By three o'clock, the sun was out, beaming golden warmth on the damp grounds. Steamy moisture snaked up from the grass. Humidity, coupled with the wet breeze off the Thames, dampened Willa's muslin gown. She fluffed out her skirt, hoping to create a drying effect, but to little avail. She was wet through and through, no help for it.

Dozens of guests gathered under Lady Tricot's enormous maroon-striped marquee and dined on her generous buffet. Those not eating gathered in Turkish tents for cards or conversation. A violinist, a mandolin player, and a flutist wandered around the grounds, playing for clusters of guests.

Willa stood beside Lady Tricot's daughter, watching a juggler spin six balls into an ever-widening circle. "Are they authentic Gypsies?"

Alfreda nodded. "Mama adheres quite strictly to her themes. She sent inquiries all over the south of England. I expect she would have shipped Romanys here from the Continent had she not heard of this troupe traveling through South Sussex. She can be quite determined once a notion takes her."

Willa glanced at the young woman she had originally thought frail and reserved. In this setting, Alfreda looked more like a powerful elfin princess. Although slender, she towered over Willa by at least six inches. Alfreda did not hunch, but carried herself with the bearing of a soldier.

"It's remarkable how different you appear when not in your mother's presence."

Alfreda smiled. "I knew at once I liked you. You do not dissemble much, do you?"

Willa adjusted her new spectacles, trying to get a clearer image of her companion's face. Alfreda did not appear to be offended. "I've been told I speak my mind too freely."

"Not for my taste. I've no patience with small talk. Drat, here come those pesky musicians again. Mother's orders, I suppose." She mimicked her mother's mannish stance. "Follow m'daughter. Play something romantic on that fiddle, d'you hear? Make the eligible men stand up and take notice, eh?"

Willa couldn't help but laugh. Alfreda's imitation was superb.

The young lady shook out her pale blue gown. "I confess, the air is so wet, I feel like I'm standing in bathwater."

Willa nodded. "Embarrassing is it not? I cannot keep my gown from sticking to me like a plaster."

Alfreda laughed. "Come, I've had enough of juggling. Shall we try our hand at archery? Mama set up targets as a small concession to me."

Willa's smile faded. If she could see the target at all it would be nothing short of a miracle. "I would very much like to try, although I must confess I have never attempted the exercise before. I wonder with my eyesight—"

"You are in luck. I am an excellent teacher and, in this muck, we're sure to be the only ones at the course."

Willa certainly hoped so. She would not like to put an arrow through an innocent bystander. With any luck, the targets would be extremely large. The size of one of Mr. Kemble's elephants would be ideal.

Sadly, they were not the size of elephants. No, not even baby elephants. The targets looked like pillows of straw, sitting atop wooden supports, with two concentric circles painted on each bag.

Willa did not need any complex calculations to predict the outcome of such an exercise. "I think I might enjoy observing you shoot rather more than participating myself."

The elfin princess made no answer; she simply strapped on a leather arm protector. Willa rightly deduced that she would not be allowed to merely watch.

Alfreda pulled back the largest of the bows and let fly her first arrow. It thwacked into the straw. Willa squinted. The shaft appeared to be sticking out of the exact center.

"Your turn," her hostess commanded.

Willa took a deep breath and tried to pull back the string of her small bow with the same prowess Alfreda had demonstrated. The arrow wobbled up. She realigned it, squinted at the target, and tilted her head to sight down the shaft, but her head bumped the string, catching a tendril of hair as she pulled back farther. She eased up on her fingers, but the string snapped forward. The arrow flew. Several strands of her hair yanked out at the same time.

Willa listened carefully for the cries of a wounded guest. The arrow might have flown anywhere. She squinted in the vicinity of the target. Not there.

Alfreda shaded her eyes with her hand. "Don't think I've ever seen a shot quite like that one."

"Where did it go?"

"Just over there." Alfreda pointed at the top of a small yellow-striped tent, where the feathered shaft of Willa's arrow shamed her by waving cheerfully in the breeze. "The fortune-teller's tent."

"Oh dear. I wonder if she predicted that?"

Alfreda laughed. "Who would have thought you could get such distance out of that little bow. The arc was quite remarkable. Showed some strength. With a little practice you might become quite good."

Willa smiled. "You are too kind. I nearly killed your fortune-teller. You might as easily conclude, England would be a safer place if I never picked up a bow again."

"No, no. It's all a matter of focusing on the goal. See what I mean?" She deftly pulled back another arrow. It whizzed straightforward and landed in the target right beside her previous arrow. "Do not think about the arrow or the bow. Concentrate only on the goal. I find this a useful stratagem in all areas of life."

"An interesting philosophy." Here was an arena in which Willa felt safe. Philosophy. She would not maim or kill anyone if she effectively distracted Alfreda with a discussion on philosophy. "How does one apply this ideology to other aspects of life? It seems quite impossible to reach a goal without first considering the means to achieving it."

The warrior elf set her weapon down on the archery table. "I will illustrate. Do you see that gentleman down by the dock on the canal?"

Willa peered in vain in the direction Alfreda indicated, but it was hopeless. "No, I'm afraid it's too far away. New glasses, but still it's all a blur." She pointed to the new spectacles her aunt had commissioned especially for her.

"It's Lord Tournsby." Alfreda tilted her head to one side and folded her arms across her chest. "A complete wastrel. My goal."

"You mean to shoot him?"

Alfreda laughed. "Not just yet. No, I mean to marry him."

"Marry?" Willa shook her head, wondering if she'd misheard. "But, I met him at the opera. I wouldn't want to disparage the fellow, but he seemed . . . You are . . . and he—"

"Yes." Alfreda nodded. "Just so. A perfect match. He hasn't a shilling to call his own. And I want nothing more than to get out from under my dear mother's thumb. A fellow like that will take my dowry, set me up in his estate, and promptly run off to Town, leaving me to do as I please. Which is exactly what I want."

Willa saw any number of flaws to this reasoning and very much wanted to enumerate them. She began with the most pressing point. "He'll exhaust your funds. You'll both end up destitute."

Her Majesty, the elf queen, arched one eyebrow. "That's the beauty of it. He can't. Entailed in a quarterly trust. My father is a very clever man. I adore him. He detests gamblers and spendthrifts. Set up my trust with ironclad caveats. My husband may use my dowry to pay off his debts if he wishes, but the living is protected. A man with very specific goals, my father."

Willa pinched up her brow. "Having a father you admire and respect so well, could you marry a man you did not?"

Alfreda shrugged. "My primary goal is to be left alone. Free to live my life as I please. I've calculated that Lord Tournsby is most likely to do just that."

"Highly probable." Willa nodded. "And so, you're focusing on your goal. But I don't understand how you expect to marry him without considering the bow that will fling you into his arms?"

Alfreda beamed. "How quick you are. That's it, precisely. I do not consider the means, only the goal. You may be certain, I will hit my mark."

"Without preparing a stratagem?"

"Exactly!"

Willa smoothed the feathers on the shaft of her arrow into perfectly even peaks. "You and my aunt have quite opposing viewpoints."

"Lady Alameda? Yes, a devious woman, I'd say. You realize she's spreading a rumor that she intends to make you her heir?"

Willa nearly dropped the arrow. "I knew she was up to something!" She glanced away, embarrassed, angry. "But why? It's patently untrue. She has no such intention."

Alfreda shrugged. "Impossible to discern Lady Alameda's motives."

"As you said, a devious woman." Willa straightened her spine and squared her shoulders. "Well, she may find herself in too deep this time. I shall set the record straight."

Alfreda handed her the bow. "Good. For I rather think Lord Tournsby has set his sights on the pot of gold he thinks you're sitting on."

"I will gladly disabuse him of that notion."

"Thank you."

Willa nocked an arrow into place, pulled back the bow, and focused on the target.

The elfin princess spoke softly. "Think only of your arrow piercing the black circle in the center of the bag."

Willa did. She was scarcely aware of releasing the arrow, barely felt the whip of the string near her cheek. She saw it before it happened, the shaft embedded in the center of the bag. Thwack. There it was. Dead center.

For a moment everything in her world tipped sideways. All of her training seemed useless. Socrates had not prepared her for this. She felt an overwhelming desire to calculate the circumference of a circle, any circle, except the one she'd just shot her arrow into. Or add up a column of figures. But someone was clapping.

She turned. Alex. Her breath caught. Although he was not clapping. He was frowning, staring with amazement at her arrow sticking out of the target. The breeze ruffled through his brown curls, and Willa labored to make her lungs perform properly.

The clapping man was his friend, Mr. Erwin. "Good show, Miss Linnet. Outstanding marksmanship. Must have been shooting since you was in leading strings."

She shook her head. "No. Never before today."

Alex came closer and scrutinized her carefully. "New spectacles?"

Willa nodded. "Yes, perhaps that explains it." But she knew in her heart it was something more, something irrational, and considerably more perplexing. She would analyze it later.

"Hmmm." Alex nodded and continued to frown skeptically. "Still. Unusually good shot."

She swallowed. "Pure luck. An anomaly. No explanation."

Alfreda made a start. "A perfectly good expl—"

"Miss Tricot, are you acquainted with my friends?" Naturally, they knew one another. All the same, they nodded and performed the expected pleasantries. Willa inhaled deeply, she did not want to discuss Alfreda's philosophy on goals, nor how one obtains objectives without really trying.

Willa adjusted her gown, which was sticking to her in a most embarrassing fashion. Drat the humidity. Drat Aunt Honore for insisting that she wear this flimsy muslin. At least it was green. She held on to the hope that the fabric could not be seen clear through. Although the weave was loose enough she could use it to strain curds. She glanced up and realized Alex was watching her adjusting the top of her gown.

The familiar hot flush rushed up into her cheeks. She sighed. "There's no hope for it, is there?"

He smiled crookedly. "Very little."

The heat in her face reached full bloom. "My aunt's choice."

"No doubt."

She was grateful he did her the service of not staring, although she wondered at his frown. Had she said something?

Dashing up from the banks of the inlet, Lord Tournsby hailed them. He arrived at the archery tables nearly out of breath. His collar points were restrictively high and his neckcloth a frothy extravagance that must surely be suffocating him. Despite all that, he bowed elegantly. "Lovely day, is it not?"

Willa watched their faces carefully as Lord Tournsby greeted his hostess's daughter. He was not unmoved by Alfreda's beauty, and she did not seem displeased with the pompous lord. The universe appeared to be completely devoid of logic or good sense today.

It did not surprise Willa that the Romany musicians arrived, rapidly fiddling. They achieved the impossible by blending a raucous jig and a love song into one melody. Willa shook her head.

Lord Tournsby turned his attention to her. "This is a happy coincidence. Just thinking how delightful it might be to sail around the inlet. Perfect day for it. Lady Tricot provided several boats down by the landing. Happy to row you?"

Harry sputtered. "What? You can't. I was just on point of asking myself."

"You may ask yourself all you like," Tournsby muttered, smiling at Willa and Alfreda. "I got the job done."

Alex put a hand on Tournsby's shoulder. "Enough boats for all of us, I imagine. Wouldn't want to miss watching you row, *Neddie,* old boy."

Tournsby grimaced.

Willa fell in with Alex's scheme. "Yes." She looped her arm around Alfreda's. "We'd all love to come." She had a counterplan of her own. So much for thinking only of the goal.

10

The Past Is But a Dream, the Future Is Uncertain

Alex had only a few moments to put his plan into action. Tournsby would not win this bout. This next parry would block the blighter's scheme completely.

Musicians followed closely on their heels, as the five companions strolled down the lawn toward the quays. The mandolin player strummed loudly and sang in his native language. His full vibrato resonated across the grounds, making it difficult to carry on a conversation.

Alex leaned close to Willa's ear. "That wouldn't be one of your arrows would it? Atop that tent?"

She nodded. "My first attempt. I'm quite relieved no one came to any harm."

He shrugged. "Are you certain? It's quite possible the fortune-teller died of heart failure. Or she may, at this very moment, be quaking in her shoes. Afraid to step foot outside her fortress for fear she is under attack."

Willa squinted up at him. "Oh, now you are bamming me." She smiled back at him. "Still. I suppose the proper thing would be to stop in and apologize."

"I'm not precisely certain what etiquette requires of you in this situation? Surely, penance of some kind." He gave her his most pinched, studious expression.

She shook her head at his mock severity. Copper corkscrew filaments fluttered out of place, and the moist air tightened each delightful little curl. He couldn't help but smile. She returned his ridiculous adoration with a frown, a pretense of annoyance. Nevertheless, he wanted to keep hold of her attention. He found he enjoyed her overserious scolding expression almost as much as he liked seeing her face filled with warmth. But instead she turned away from him to Alfreda, and expressed her wish to visit the Gypsy's unfortunate tent.

Harry, of course, threw up a huzzah. "Great fun, the fortune-teller. Want *my* palm read, as well."

Willa shook her head. "I don't wish to have my fortune told. No, indeed, I merely want to apologize for frightening her." She leveled her instructress gaze on poor Harry. "Beyond a matter of a few simple probabilities, it's very unscientific to assume anyone can predict the future."

"What? All in the spirit of fun," Harry sputtered, adjusting his cravat, which had wilted into a hopeless puddle in the humidity. "Can't visit the Gypsy without having your fortune told. Wouldn't be the thing. No, must do it."

Alex watched with interest as Harry struggled to persuade her.

Willa made an effort to console the flustered fellow, patting his arm. "You must, of course, have your palm read if it amuses you. I have no wish to be a killjoy."

"Not killing my joy. No. Sterner stuff than that. Bit of fun, that's all." Harry cast a pleading look in Alex's direction while flapping the unbuttoned sides of his coat to generate a breeze.

Tournsby hissed at him under his breath. "You're not a duck, Harry. Leave your coat be."

"Just trying to drum up some air. Wet to the bone and hotter than old Ned."

Tournsby addressed the ladies. "I agree wholeheartedly with Miss Linnet. No one can predict my future better than I. And for the nonce, I predict a delightful afternoon out on the Thames. Think of the breeze on the river. Wouldn't boating be far more refreshing than a visit to the Gypsy?"

Harry realized his strategic error. "Not that hot. No. See here, I've stopped fanning. Cool as a day in May. Best to visit the palm reader."

Neddie's self-satisfied expression made Alex want to knock him down.

Alex struggled to keep the irritation out of his tone. "Seems to me, Harry is merely allowing for the plight of the Gypsy. He's suggesting we pay for a reading, as an apology for putting an arrow through her tent, isn't that right, Harry?"

"Oh, yes. Yes. That's it."

"But it's my mother's tent," Alfreda explained.

Alex smiled calmly; apparently scheming required more effort than he'd anticipated. "Yes, of course, I meant as amends for the fright it caused the poor woman."

"Might be a man," Tournsby offered, grinning sourly as if he suspected Alex was up to something.

"Shall we see?" Alex held open the tent flap.

Five of them in the tent made for a muggy crush. Alex propelled Willa to the front, where she came face-to-face with the Romany woman.

"Oh my." Willa's voice caught.

Alex understood her astonishment and placed his hand on her back for support.

The Gypsy was perfectly designed for the role of fortune-teller. The loss of one eye made her frightening, while at the same time her startling features compelled one to look at her. She'd been beautiful once, this woman. Now, age crumpled her spine and drew her dark olive skin into rivulets. Yet, her thick hair, whether by nature or artifice, remained black as coal. Her seeing eye was as yellow as a cat's.

"So, yer the young lady what nearly sent me to an early grave."

"Yes. I mean, no. I intended no harm. The arrow went astray, you see. I'm dreadfully sorry."

Willa's heart was pounding so loudly Alex thought he could almost hear it from where he stood. But of course he couldn't. He could only see her breasts rising and falling—and what was he doing watching her bosom as if it mattered. He had a task at hand. He would see to it, and be done with this charade.

Willa's back felt damp under his hand. Her gown was nearly soaked through. Small consequence if she did go for an unexpected dunking in the Thames. Maybe he was wasting his time, thwarting Tournsby's plans. Still, if she drowned, he would have to shoot the reckless scoundrel, and that might prove bothersome, laws being what they are and all. He lowered his hand to the curve of her waist. Drier there. Smoother. So soft. A sensuous arc that fit his hand perfectly. He could almost feel her skin through the fabric. She looked up at him, questioning, not scolding, inquisitive. Gad, he was pawing her right here in front of everyone. He let go immediately.

The old woman dragged Willa away from him. "Come, I'll tell ye yer future."

Willa protested, but the Gypsy prevailed. The two of them sat at a small table, and the others gathered around. Alex stood back, near the entrance of the tent. The heat was stifling. He needed to breathe. Thank God it would all be over soon. Willa would be safe, and he could take leave of this wretched party.

The Gypsy took out a purple silk bag and poured salt into Willa's palm, instructing her to turn it out onto the table. Once the salt was strewn, the old woman studied the spill as if it were a priceless painting. She traced the edges of the pattern with her gnarled fingers.

"Stick out yer tongue," she ordered and placed several grains on the end of Willa's tongue. "Close yer eyes."

Alex didn't expect Willa to comply so readily, but she did. He moved closer to watch.

"Tell me what ye taste," the soothsayer demanded.

"Salt."

"No. Concentrate. Seek other flavors."

Willa closed her eyes tighter. "Perhaps you've inadvertently mixed a grain of sugar into your salt. There is a faint sweetness."

Alex smiled. Little Miss Logical had discerned the Romany's game.

The old soothsayer nodded. "Sweetness? Eh? Very good. Anything else?"

"Lemon. And something quite bitter I cannot identify." She opened her eyes.

The one-eyed woman stared at Willa as if she could see into her soul. After an interminably long pause, she nodded sagely. "I will tell ye what it means."

Tournsby snorted and muttered, "Go ahead then, get on with it."

Harry poked him in the arm and shushed him. "Don't disrupt the forces."

Tournsby snorted again.

The fortune-teller spread her hands and indicated the wave of salt strewn on the table. "I see danger. Mortal danger."

Willa squinted. "You surmise that from lemon-flavored salt?"

The fortune-teller traced the jagged perimeter of the spatter. "No. The bitter taste. It foretells of impending death."

Harry gasped. "Ods bodkins! No need to go that far. Surely, *all* salt is bitter. What?"

The old woman shrugged and dragged her fingers through the spill, making four even lines. "I can only tell you what I see. I see water."

She shut her yellow eye. Her head lolled back. "Dark waves lapping, splashing, closing over ye head. Bubbles trickling out of ye mouth, as ye sink down, *down* into the depths. Strangling!" Her hands went to her own throat. "Brown river water choking the life out of ye."

The Gypsy jolted forward, eye wide open, and clutched Willa's hand in her twisted claw. In a whispered hiss she warned, "Stay away from the water!"

Willa swallowed hard and shook her head. Her voice cracked as she tried to raise it above a startled whisper. "No. I don't believe any of this. Flummery. All of it. Nonsense."

Harry sputtered and chafed his hands together. "Don't believe I want my palm read after all."

Tournsby glared at Alex.

Alex shrugged.

Alfreda patted Willa's shoulder and urged her up from the chair. "Come on. Bound to be a hoax. Let's go outside and get some fresh air, shall we?"

"Just so. Never heard such folderol." Tournsby threw back the flap and led the women out into the sunlight.

Alex waited until they had all left the tent before sliding two silver coins onto the fortune-teller's table. "A bit drastic, don't you think?"

"Not easily convinced, that one."

Alex sighed. "I suppose not."

"Pity I couldn't tell 'er the truth. Seen a vision of 'er trapped in the arms of that other one, the dark-haired dandy. Better off drowning, if anyone was to ask me."

Alex tried to school his features. He would not react. "He paid you to say that."

"Not he." She shook her head, silk swishing and bells tinkling. "Not he." She cackled.

Alex stormed out of the tent and nearly collided with Lady Alameda and Lord Monmouth. Lady Alameda quizzed him with a mere lift of her brow, goading and questioning in one efficient gesture. He didn't have time to satisfy her curiosity, nor did he have the patience for her bear-baiting.

He made a swift bow and hurried to catch up with Willa before Tournsby talked her into a rowboat.

11

Rub a Dub Dub, Who's in the Tub?

Willa and Alfreda strolled arm in arm down the hillside toward the water. Lord Tournsby prattled on beside them, and Mr. Erwin stumbled along in the rear, huffing and puffing. In the distance, the Thames moved like a colossal brown snake sliding swiftly but silently through the grassy lowlands.

Willa wondered, fleetingly, if the Gypsy was right. Would the snake suffocate her? Would she be pulled under the murky water, the life sucked out of her? But, no! She mentally tore herself away from such morbid imaginings, and nodded at Lord Tournsby, although she wasn't attending to his words. She needed to calculate. She could deduce only two explanations for the Gypsy's grim prediction. Revenge for the arrow was plausible, but unlikely. Yet, that seemed to be Lord Tournsby's prime theory.

The other possibility baffled her. What was Alex playing at? Why had he held her so fondly, touched her so intimately, and transformed her mind into useless soup? But of course, men like Alex knew exactly how to turn women into muddled idiots. But why her?

And why would he want to keep her out of the water? Unless . . . She took a closer look at Lord Tournsby as he expounded on his hypothesis a trifle too zealously.

". . . Annoyed because you frightened her. It's quite possible, your arrow scared away one of her more affluent customers."

So, that was it. Willa smiled. She glanced back up the hill to the fortune-teller's yellow-striped tent to see if Alex was coming. If she had assessed the situation correctly, he would be. And so he was. She grinned. Had he truly gone to such lengths to look out for her? An extraordinary kindness, or was it? Could he have another motive? Dare she hope? No, that was far too optimistic a stance. Unthinkable. A rake like Alex? She watched him stride down the hill, so handsome, so confident, the very picture of one of Miss Edgewater's heroes. But that was nonsense. She should never have read any of those silly books. No, it was merely kindness on his part. But oh, if only he weren't a rake.

She turned away. "What say you, Alfreda? Revenge or a jest?"

Alfreda's arm was still looped around Willa's. She smiled serenely. "All a hum. Not worried a bit. Concentrating on my goal." She winked.

To Willa's amazement Tournsby was actually listening. "And what goal might that be?"

Alfreda stopped short and gazed at him levelly. For a moment, Willa was afraid the forthright elfin princess would tell him exactly who and what her goal was. The silence began to tick loudly. Willa tugged on her friend's arm.

Tournsby looked away, ostensibly to adjust the lace at his cuff. "Beg pardon. Didn't mean to intrude."

Alfreda's pale blue eyes would unnerve anyone, especially when focused so intently, as they were on her prey. "Someday, I give you my word, my lord, I will tell you. But, not today."

Tournsby swallowed, not appearing quite as cynical and self-assured as normal.

Harry shuffled up, short of breath from the hike downhill. "Tell him what?" He glanced from one to the other, completely baffled.

Fortunately, Alex caught up with them before anyone had to explain. "Not still going rowing, are you?"

Willa could not repress her delight. "Yes. Absolutely. Terribly nice day for it."

"But?" His expression was well worth the price she'd paid of being frightened by the fortune-teller.

She smiled. "Oh yes. The Gypsy convinced me. I'm normally quite nervous on the water. Might not have gone in at all. But, when she told me I would drown—I realized, I mustn't live my life in fear."

"You're afraid of water?" The incredulity on Alex's face made Willa want to burst into laughter.

"No longer." She held a finger over her lips, trying to hide her mirth.

"But—"

Alfreda cut in. "Unlikely anyone would drown here, anyway. The current from the Thames into the canal is fairly moderate. And the pond is scarcely deep enough to accommodate a large boat."

"Excellent. There you have it. Shall we?" Tournsby led the group onto a small pier.

Willa whispered to Alfreda, "Do you swim? I fear we are in for a dunking."

"Passably." Alfreda nodded conspiratorially.

The planks creaked as Harry thumped onto the dock, charging ahead of Tournsby. "I'll row," he offered.

Lord Tournsby frowned. "Now, Harry, wouldn't want to put you to that much exercise. Harder than you think, rowing."

"No, no. Insist upon it. You and the ladies must enjoy the scenery. Nothing to it. I'll do the work."

Without waiting for further argument, Harry clambered into the waiting boat and took up the oars on the aft seat. Lord Tournsby climbed into the bow and steadied the craft while Willa and Alfreda gingerly stepped into the soggy boat and took their places on the center plank, leaving the small rung on the bow for Lord Tournsby. He made a fuss of adjusting the seat.

He straightened up and slapped his hand against the piling as if he had just remembered something. "Afraid there's only room for four, Alex, *old chum.*" He grinned, appearing quite pleased with himself.

Alex made no reply. The muscles in his jaw contracted markedly as he stood with lips pressed together.

"Here. Hold this for me, will you?" Tournsby handed him something and chuckled as he untied the bowline.

"Wait!" Willa stood up suddenly. The dinghy rocked as she reached out to the pier. "I can't do it. I changed my mind. Help me out."

"What?" Lord Tournsby turned, his mouth hanging open.

Alex grabbed her hands and pulled her up onto the dock just as the rowboat drifted away from dock. Tournsby plopped down to keep from losing his balance, as Harry thrust in the paddles and propelled them away from the shore.

"Safe journey." Alex grinned.

Willa stood beside him and waved. Difficult to pretend innocence, when one is terribly guilty of such delicious mischief. She'd never done anything as deceptive as this in her entire life. And it was all his fault.

When the rowing party had paddled a few yards out, she whispered softly but firmly to the culprit, "Kindly tell your friends that the rumors are not true. My aunt has no intention of leaving me her estate. I am not her heir. Nor do I have even the smallest expectation in that quarter."

Alex turned to her, clearly taken aback. It gratified her that he didn't say something absurd like, *Whatever can you mean?* He nodded and exhaled slowly. "I've already told them as much. I'm afraid they refuse to believe me."

"You did." She felt pleased that he'd seen through her aunt's ploy and tried to protect her.

"Yes, but Tournsby cannot be persuaded."

"In that case, I will simply have to tell him myself." She glanced at the rowboat out on the pond. "Punctured the hull, did he?"

Alex stared at her. She watched him puzzling it all out, adding up what she had guessed, until it all fit into a tidy column of calculable figures. "I suppose so. But how did you know?"

"A few simple deductions."

He moved nearer. The warmth of his body, the strength of his being curled around her like an invisible fortress. Would he kiss her again? But no, of course not, that was out of the question, more foolishness.

He opened his hand near her breast. A fat cork stopper lay in his palm. "He handed me this, just before you abandoned ship."

"Yes, Alfreda noticed him down by the docks earlier. Plugging up his hole until the crucial moment, no doubt. I must say, it's not very original of him."

"No." Alex chuckled softly. "Don't think he was aiming for originality. I expect he entertained visions of you swooning in his arms, overcome with gratitude after he rescued you from the river."

"He didn't think I'd notice a contrived leak?"

Alex leaned closer and crooked up that deadly half grin that always made her legs feel weak. "Poor nitwit. He didn't realize he was up against Copernicus and Galileo. Had the mistaken idea you were an unexceptional sort of chit."

A compliment? She hoped so. Must have been, because suddenly her damp gown and sodden slippers evaporated, and she felt pleasant and warm and . . . and what lunacy was she giving in to now?

She dove for a distraction. "I can't abide that word. Chit. Sounds like something that fell off a teacup."

"Begging your pardon. It will never pass my lips again." He reached for her hand and placed it on his arm. "Now tell me, what gave me away? The fortune-teller, wasn't it?"

She smiled and nodded.

"Blast! Oh, begging your pardon again." He bowed his head, but his wicked smile belied any act of contrition. "Knew it was doing it up a bit brown. But, on such short notice, it was the only scheme I could invent to keep you out of the cursed boat."

"You could've just told me." She returned his gaze evenly.

He had the good sense to look properly chagrined. "Never thought of that." He chuckled and patted her hand.

"Nevertheless, I thank you. It was a noble gesture."

He stiffened. "Nothing to do with nobility. No. I told you before, I'm not . . . No. Simply trying to spike Neddie's guns that's all."

"Oh, of course you were! How silly of me." She fluttered a hand to her breast just as she had seen Honore do when playing coy. "What could I have been thinking? It wasn't noble of you, to keep me from being rescued by a lord. Never mind that he's a penniless fortune hunter. Small matter that I cannot swim one whit, and might have drowned. No, you are right. I might've snagged a title." Too bad she didn't have a fan. She could have put more of Honore's lessons to use and rapped his arm saucily. Instead, she had to content herself with fixing him with a scolding frown. "Reprehensible. That's what it was."

He nodded, considerably more relaxed. "Precisely."

Too bad she hadn't a jot or tittle within her whole being that truly felt like scolding him. She wanted more than anything in the world to hug him and tell him thank you, a *thank you* he would believe.

Instead, she stood contently at his side, watching the rowboat trundle down the canal to the pond. There had never been a more pleasant day in all of her memories. Alex toyed with her hand as he held it in the crook of his arm. The sun warmed her neck, and the strength she felt in his forearm played havoc with her senses.

Perplexing. That a man with no ambition and reckless morals should elicit such emotion from her, while a staid, reliable man like Sir Daniel did not. It was not logical. But today she would abandon logic. Just for today.

Willa glanced up at him. Had she the luxury, she would stand beside him for the rest of her days. But Alex Braeburn would not be wandering through her days for much longer. He had a life apart from her, a life with other women, beautiful women, with veils and coins in their navels. Emptiness thudded into her stomach, and it was not from hunger.

"Bad business that," Alex said, almost as if he could read her mind. He gestured toward the pond. "Harry's rowed them away from the shore. I'm not certain he can swim outside a bathtub. What about your friend?"

"Alfreda? I would be utterly astonished were she not a most capable swimmer. Seems to be competent at nearly everything. By the by, you might mention to Lord Tournsby that *she does* have a rather handsome dowry."

Willa shaded her eyes to get a better look at the hapless trio. "I cannot see well, but it's beginning to sink, isn't it?"

Alex nodded. "I should think so. Looks quarter full to me. It's sitting low, but if they row hard, they might just make it to shore without a soaking."

Tournsby gesticulated wildly at poor Harry, pointing toward the shore and waving his arm at the hull.

"Looks like Harry tried to turn the craft, but he miscalculated which oar to put to." Alex shook his head. "They're moving farther from shore. Of all the—now what's Tournsby doing?"

Willa squinted. Lord Tournsby stood up, precariously making his way to the back of the boat. The vessel rocked from side to side, especially when he tried to step around Alfreda. "What's he doing?"

"Looks like the dunderhead wants to take the oars from Harry. Your friend's arguing with him about it. Can't blame her."

Willa could hear bits and pieces of Alfreda's heated warning floating across the water. But evidently Lord Tournsby had lost patience. He abruptly stepped over her seat.

"He's going to sink them." Willa grimaced.

Alex nodded. "Yes, but not intentionally this time, I think." He gripped Willa's hand, tense, as they observed Tournsby's blunder.

Devoid of weight, the bow of the little craft tipped up.

"Call for help!" Alex took off, running along the edge of the canal toward the inlet.

Alfreda lurched forward, trying to correct the distribution, but her small contribution did little to offset Tournsby and Harry's combined weight in the aft. The prow lifted high into the air. Water rushed into the stern. Harry jumped up. Alfreda and Tournsby were both thrown from the boat. Nose up, it sank into the brown water.

Willa yelled for help and waved her arms, pointing, calling attention to the accident until servants and guests started running down the hill toward them. Then she dashed after Alex.

Alfreda surfaced, her white hair easy to spot. She swam with long capable strokes, just as Willa had expected she would. Amazing girl.

But Harry appeared to be caught in an undercurrent. He splashed and flapped at the water to no avail. He bobbed like a cork, as the current carried him out of the pond and down the canal.

"He'll be carried out to the river!" Willa shouted to Alex up ahead.

Alex glanced up as he yanked off his shoes and stockings. He acknowledged Harry's predicament with a nod, but pointed to Tournsby, who was floating facedown. "Must've hit his head!"

"Alfreda!" Willa screamed. "Freda! Look behind you!"

The elfin warrioress glanced up, saw Willa point,

and immediately turned around, swimming to Tournsby's side. Without squandering a single moment on panic, Alfreda efficiently flipped him over, grasped his collar and dragged him toward shore.

Willa ran toward them, crashing through the reeds and grass. She arrived at Alex's side just as he and Alfreda hauled Tournsby out of the water. "I can help here. Poor Harry's headed out to sea. He'll be drowned."

Alex dashed off before she even finished speaking. He raced to the far side of the pond, where the ebbing current was picking up speed and carrying Harry down the canal toward the Thames.

Alex grabbed a paddle from a moored rowboat and threw himself onto the end of a pier, extending the oar far out into the water. "Harry! Grab hold!"

Harry fumbled, but finally made purchase. He clutched the paddle as if it were his long-lost mother, and Alex dragged him to safety.

Willa breathed a sigh of relief as she helped pull Lord Tournsby well up onto the lawn. Alfreda shoved back her sopping hair. Droplets sprayed over Willa and their unconscious patient.

"Help me turn him on his side," Alfreda commanded. Drenched, but just as single-minded as when dry, the mighty Alfreda delivered a powerful blow to the center of Lord Tournsby's back. "Can't let him die. He's perfect." She whacked him again.

His lordship belched up a tankard of muddy water. He wasn't done there. He spewed up breakfast and lake weeds in a gushing slurry of fishy water. *Perfect.*

12

Jack Fell Down and Broke His Crown

Alex stood beside an enormous fireplace inside one of Lady Tricot's spacious guest rooms attempting to dry his river-stained shirt. His cravat had been rinsed out by a servant and now hung over the fender, steaming from the heat of the fire, tainting the air with the smell of musty lake water and cooked cotton. His coat had been carried off to parts unknown for a proper cleaning.

Harry huddled in a chair by the fire, wearing a dressing gown, and downing his fourth snifter of brandy. "Could've been killed. Demmed lucky, that's what. Even luckier you were there to tow me in. Could've been the end of me. Might've stuck my spoon in the wall."

"Not a bit of it." Alex pressed a reassuring hand on Harry's shoulder. "Given another yard or two, you'd have paddled out on your own. I'm certain of it."

Harry shook his head. "Don't know. Have a look at Neddie. Might've been me. If only I'd rowed closer to shore like he asked. All my fault."

"An accident, Harry. No point in blaming yourself."

Poor Harry, wide-eyed and still shaking like an old

woman, gravity didn't suit him. If he drank much more he would, most likely, end up as unconscious as Tournsby.

The waterlogged lord lay moaning softly in the luxurious snowy folds of a large four-poster bed. His pallor remained a disconcerting shade of gray, and Alex didn't like the look of the bruise swelling out like an apricot and turning an ugly raspberry hue.

Lady Tricot bustled into the room without a thought for any of the gentlemen's state of dishabille. A small cavalcade of servants followed her, like chicks trailing behind a giant mother quail. They fluffed Tournsby's pillows, checked the temperature of his feet, straightened the bedclothes, and waited for instructions.

The hulking matron turned to Alex. "He may yet survive. Sent for my physician. Most fortunate my daughter pulled him out when she did." She clucked her tongue. "Dreadful business. Ought not be moved. We'll attend to his needs until he recovers."

Alex bowed his head. "Very gracious of you, my lady. Lord Tournsby will, undoubtedly, be most grateful."

"Hhhm, yes. *If* he recovers." She shook her head as if it were only a vague possibility. "Well, must return to my other guests." Lady Tricot glanced skeptically back at the bed before abruptly exiting the room.

In the ensuing silence, Alex stretched out in an armchair in front of the blaze. He'd finally begun to relax when a young footman brought him a pair of folded notes.

"I was told to give you these, sir. Although, this one is for the red-haired miss." He nodded toward the hallway where Willa and Alfreda had been ushered to dry their gowns. "I can take it directly to her if you prefer.

But her aunt said you would know how to advise the young lady."

Alex frowned and took both of the missives.

The footman bowed at the waist. "As to the other note, sir, a local lad waits in the kitchens for your reply."

Alex hesitated for only a second before flipping open the unsealed note from Lady Alameda.

My dear Wilhemina,

Delightful spectacle. Your friends must be congratulated. Covent Garden pales in comparison. However, now that the entertainment is over, the party has turned deadly dull. Monmouth and I are taking our leave.

You may send for my coach if you wish, but I recommend you apply to Mr. Erwin for an escort home. I'm certain your friend, Mr. Braeburn, is in a better position to advise you than I, but I believe young Erwin is fairly well-situated, several thousand pounds per annum. Seems a biddable sort of fellow. With proper handling he might be trained not to squander it all at the clubs.

Do as you wish, my dear. I, however, do not expect to return home until midday tomorrow or the next.

—Adieu,
Yr Beloved Aunt

He reread it twice, and shook his head. *Of all the conniving, manipulative, galling* . . . He swore aloud.

Lady Alameda's improper conduct toward her niece was beyond reckless. It bordered on insanity. He slapped the letter down on the side table and promptly picked it up again.

How could she have so little regard for her niece's welfare? Such folly might well ruin an innocent young woman like Willa. Had this odious note been sent to another man, he might have taken full advantage of the situation. How dare Lady Alameda presume he would advise Willa concerning Harry. Utter lunacy. Completely irresponsible.

And yet, who was he to criticize? His father's epithets lashed across his mind, *wastrel, scapegrace, ne'r-do-well.*

Alex glanced over at Harry who, at last, had stopped shaking. The exhausted fellow sat with his head propped in one hand, the empty snifter in the other, his dressing gown gaping open over his protruding white belly as he dozed. *This* was the paragon Lady Alameda suggested Willa might trust to convey her home, perhaps, even make a husband. Alex liked Harry, but the thought of Willa taking the silly coxcomb into her bed roiled in his gut as if he'd eaten a bad fish.

After today, seeing her in a damp gown, he could all too easily envision each sensuous curve of her body. Curves nature could not possibly intend for Harry's chubby hands. Nor Tournsby's stealthy tapered fingers. Decidedly not.

Alex stood up abruptly, and threw the crumpled letter into the fire. "Tell the housekeeper I'll need my coat as soon as possible. She needn't bother about the stains."

The footman nodded. "And the other note, sir? What shall I tell the lad?"

He'd nearly forgotten the other missive. He picked it up from the side table, flipped it open, and took a deep breath. "Have him ready the gig."

Alfreda and Willa peeked into the room just as the footman hurried out. Willa had exchanged her wet mud-splattered gown for a more serviceable brown dress, obviously lent to her by Alfreda, too long and too tight across the bodice. Copper and wood, a deer at sunset, her hair glowed like fire and turned the otherwise ordinary brown into a vibrant color. It took him a moment before he realized she was asking him something. He rubbed his neck.

She asked again. "How is Lord Tournsby?"

"See for yourselves." He waved at the bed.

Alfreda brushed past Willa, rushing to Tournsby's bedside, assessing the damage.

"And Harry?" Willa asked, staring at the poor sod slouched in the chair.

Alex exhaled loudly. "As well as can be expected."

She nodded. "Perhaps you might secure his robe around him. Poor fellow ought to keep warm after that dunking in the cold water."

"How very tender," Alex muttered to himself and brusquely tucked the dressing gown over Harry. "I've had a note from your aunt."

"Oh?" She glanced around the room looking for it.

Naturally, she would expect him to show it to her. He glanced at the fire. Too late for that. Her gaze followed his and undoubtedly observed the blackened wad of paper as it crackled and snaked with fiery orange ridges, sending featherweight sparks floating up the flue. He cleared his throat. "She and Lord Monmouth have been called away. Asked me to escort you home."

"Oh." She blinked. He watched her ticking through her questions and forming incorrect conclusions. Why had her aunt abandoned her? Why had he burnt the note? Finally, she looked up at him chagrined, and he felt a cad for not handling it better.

She stopped biting the corner of her lip. "She ought not to have troubled you. I can—"

"No." He forestalled her. "No trouble. But, if you would ready yourself quickly, I'd be most grateful. We must make a stop at a nearby farm." He held up the other note. "One of my horses is about to foal and evidently the farrier is away at another farm."

Alfreda called to them from Tournsby's bedside. "He's awake!"

They rushed to the bed. Tournsby's color was much improved, and his eyelids fluttered open. Alex nodded, relieved. "Looks like he'll make it. Welcome back to the land of the living, Neddie."

Tournsby moaned and tried to sit up. "Feel wretched."

Alfreda gently pushed him back down. "Lie still. You've had a nasty bump on the head. The doctor will be here shortly."

Alex folded his arms across his chest. "Regrettably, I must take my leave. Darley's Lass is about to drop her foal. But Harry is right here at your side. Ready to do your every bidding. Aren't you, Harry?"

"What? What?" Harry sputtered, and came awake, rising from his chair. "Oh. Right you are. Won't leave his side." Harry stumbled, with tousled hair, and reeking of brandy, to the other side of the bed and plopped down, jarring the mattress and the patient's head. "Till death do us part."

"Gad. I hope not," moaned Tournsby. He pressed his lips together and tried to hold back the tide rising from his stomach. Alfreda anticipated his need, and presented him with the chamberpot, stoically holding it while he wretched.

Harry, blissfully unconcerned, curled up on the far side of the bed and struck up an accompanying chorus of guttural snores.

Alex chastised himself for letting the young puppy drink so much. Blessedly, the maid arrived with Alex's coat. He tipped the servant, shrugged into the damp, dark blue superfine, and firmly guided Willa out of the room.

13

They Sailed Away in a Silver Cup Upon a Grassy Sea

It was late afternoon by the time Alex and Willa slipped away from Lady Tricot's breakfast party. The day turned unseasonably warm. Side by side they sat on the narrow driver's seat of a dogcart, a small rig in dire need of new springs, if indeed, it had ever had any in the first place. Directly behind them, the stable boy stood on the rear bench, holding the side rails like a brave Roman charioteer as they bumped and bounced over the rutted roads.

Although the cart needed refurbishing, the horse pulling it was a fine, sturdy animal, quite capable of maintaining the pace Alex set for him, a pace more suited to a mail coach. Willa felt as if her teeth were about to rattle loose.

She clutched the side of the cart, hoping they would not hit a hole in the road. If they did, surely they would all spill out into the ditch. "It's quite serious then?"

He nodded without looking at her. "Almost there."

Fast approaching them from the other end of the small lane was a cumbersome old black coach swaying ominously with a heavy load. The top deck appeared to be crammed with men. Two more men clinging on to the rear, leaned out, peering down the road as the rickety coach barreled toward Alex and Willa. Both drivers were obliged to pull up short. Alex steered as near to the edge of the road as possible, without tumbling the cart into the culvert.

"Hallooo, Mr. Braeburn!" The large man driving the coach hailed them.

Alex frowned and tipped his hat. "Squire. What's amiss?"

"Bit of bad news." The dust from both vehicles caught up to them and caused him to cough as he pointed off to the east. "Fire at the old Ridley estate."

Willa tried to make out a plume of smoke in the distance, but could see nothing save dust and the nearby trees.

"Afraid I've got to take all available men with me," the squire shouted. "Darley's Lass is in her stall. Must be off. Can't let the fire blow this way. Could lose m'barley field. Or worse." He hefted the reins. "Tommy, you attend to Mr. Braeburn. And, lad, mind the other mares as well. The almanac warned me to stay abed today." He maneuvered the cumbersome old coach around them, grumbling loudly. "Full moon. Every mare in the northern hemisphere will likely drop her foal tonight."

Alex saluted and flicked the traces. Willa saw by the hard set of his jaw that he was uneasy.

"Can you see the fire from here?" She strained to identify anything on the horizon, but it was hopeless. "Is it very bad?"

He tilted his chin in the direction the squire had

pointed. "A good six or seven miles away. Still, I don't like it. After Darley foals, I'd better lend a hand."

"I'm sorry to be a nuisance." Although she knew very well she was a hindrance, she did not wish to be anywhere else but at his side. She did not care about the jarring ride, or the dust, or the threat of fire. She was perfectly happy sitting next to him.

He clucked his tongue at the horse to quicken its pace. "As it turns out, I may stand in need of your assistance. Squire Harley has several mares of his own ready to foal. If he is right about the full moon, we may find ourselves excessively busy this evening."

The squire's stables were as lovely as any Willa could imagine. They were very modern, built of a lovely light buff red brick. Three large menacing cats guarded the arched entry. A gray-striped feline ventured forward to inspect Willa, winding around her skirts and crisscrossing her path as Willa tried to follow Alex.

They walked down a cobbled passage between the rows of stalls. Although the building was cool and shadowed, she could see that Squire Harley required that it be kept extraordinarily clean. Buckets and shovels stood neatly stacked at regular intervals, fresh straw lay on the floor of the stalls, but was brushed away from the walkway. Several of the compartments were empty. The horses occupying the remainder shuffled toward their wooden gates to scrutinize the visitors.

Alex whistled softly through his front teeth as he strode purposefully to one of the enclosures on the right side. There was an eager answering whicker.

A tall red horse stuck her head over the wooden

gate and tossed her head at him, as if scolding him for being late. When the mare caught sight of Willa, her eyes rolled back, her ears pricked up, and she pulled her head high and away from the opening.

Alex signaled for Willa to halt. "She's afraid. Let me calm her down before you come any nearer."

Willa edged away and watched with interest as he crooned to his horse.

"Ho there, girl. Steady now. It's me. Your best beau." Darley's Lass tossed her head, and came warily toward him. "That's it." Alex stroked her muzzle. "What's wrong, eh? Aren't you ready to let this youngster see the sunshine? Must do it sometime, old girl." He quietly lifted the latch. "Let's check your progress, shall we."

The stable lad stood beside Willa in the dim light of the corridor. They both held their breath as Alex eased into the box with the skittish mare. He left the door ajar. Alex moved very slowly, standing tall and erect with one hand on her at all times. She nuzzled his shoulder and made a low moaning whinny that even Willa recognized as a sound of discomfort. Alex nodded. "Yes. Any time now, and it'll be all over. I wish I could make it easier for you, Darley."

She pawed the ground and turned toward him, which prevented him from inspecting her hindquarters more thoroughly. The mare followed the sound of his soothing voice and nudged at his coat.

He opened the pocket. "No apples or carrots today I'm afraid. You wouldn't want one anyway. Not in your condition." He patted her side and slowly wended his way toward her thighs. "That's my girl, hold steady."

He smoothed one hand down her underbelly and checked her teats. "Soon, very soon, eh?" He gently lifted her tail. Darley shifted her weight and pawed the straw again. "Easy, girl." Alex moved back to her neck. "You're in fine fettle." Patting her, he reassured the pregnant mare as affectionately as a parent would an ailing child.

Willa smiled wistfully. She could not remember such moments with her mother or father. Had her mother's voice soothed her to sleep when she was ill? Had her father calmed her fears after a bad dream? Surely, they had. But she could not remember.

Alex's compassion for Darley resonated deeply within her, opening up a Pandora's box in Willa's heart. She'd never realized how much she yearned for that kind of tenderness. Someone to dote on her. But that was silly. Preposterous. A selfish desire. She banished it back into the box from which it had escaped. Trouble was, now she knew the yearning hidden there.

Alex dusted off his hands as he walked toward them. "Well, she's no longer waxing. She's dripping. This is her fifth foal. I suppose, it's not uncommon."

Tommy nodded in agreement. "Seen it afore, sir."

Alex studied the cobbled bricks on the floor for a moment. "Even so, it doesn't seem quite right. She didn't do this last time. When did the farrier say he would return?"

"Dunno, sir. 'E's tendin' 'is Grace's mares. Squire is right. Seems like every mare in the county 'as decided 'er time is up."

Alex exhaled loudly. "Very well. Keep a close eye on Darley. I'll show Miss Linnet my other horses. Then I'll introduce her to Mrs. Bennet." He turned to Willa. "The squire's amiable housekeeper. I fear you won't be very comfortable waiting with me out here in the stables."

The stable boy shuffled impatiently and glanced

down the hall toward another stall. "You'll find Midnight and his brothers running in the pasture just north of the gardens. I'd best be checkin' on t'other mares, sir."

"Certainly. But don't forget to find me immediately if there's any change. *Any* change."

The boy pulled on his forelock and hurried off.

Willa accepted Alex's arm as they walked out. "Alex, it is kind of you to think of my comfort, but I really don't wish to go to the house. I would much rather stay here, with you, to see Darley's baby born. I've never watched a horse give birth. I should like it very much."

He sighed and shook his head. "No, we've pushed the bounds of propriety nearly out of reach as it is. I ought not."

"Oh, Alex. It isn't as if I'm some sort of prize on the marriage mart that fears ruination. All these cumbersome rules are for silly girls in white dresses. It's enough to strangle the life out of a sensible woman. I've done as I pleased, gone anywhere I wished, since I was out of leading strings."

"Ah, yes, rational, logical Willa." He smiled crookedly, and she felt he was mocking her. "Do you not realize how well you were protected within the confines of St. Cleve? The whole village played nursemaid to the vicar's baby sister. Surely you see the difference? This is London. One must follow the rules or face censure."

"I hardly think anyone will censure me for observing a horse give birth."

He patted her hand. "Unfortunately, I've heard of ladies censured for far less."

Willa sniffed indignantly. "Well, this is the country. No one with any sense will care."

"Ah, there's the rub, my dear Miss Logical, we may hope for good sense, but sadly, there is very little to be found."

She decided a change of subject might be her best tactic. Nothing short of an edict from Prince George would compel her to leave Alex's side and miss out on the prospect of new life. "What lovely gardens."

"Hhmm." He peered at her suspiciously. "Yes. Lovely."

"It looks amazingly hardy, does it not?"

"Very neatly done. Nevertheless, you are still going up to the house later."

She smiled cheerfully. "You must tell me how he achieved such phenomenal growth. My brother, and yours, would be most interested."

He chuckled softly. "Very well. Harley idolizes Thomas Coke. Indeed, he proses on endlessly about Coke's brilliant innovations in farming. Very efficient, or so he tells me. And I must credit the good squire for having remarkably productive harvests. His fields yield twice that of any of his neighbors."

They came to a stile at the far end of the garden. Alex climbed to the top and stood for a moment, looking out to the east.

The lowering sun outlined his profile in gold as he studied the horizon. "Can you see it then? The fire?"

He reached down to help her up onto the top stair beside him. He stepped down on the opposite side so that they were of the same height. "There." He pointed, directing her gaze, his cheek next to hers. "Through that gap in the trees. Down the hill. Do you see the flames and smoke?"

"I can't," she whispered, loath to disturb their closeness with speech.

"There's a flicker of orange down there. And a gray

cloud rising just above the trees. Can you not see the smoke?"

His hair brushed against her cheek. He smelled perfectly wonderful, like brandy and soap and . . . and vaguely of fish water from the river. It didn't matter. Altogether, he smelled perfect. Just as a man ought. "Uh hum," she murmured happily, absurdly, as if they weren't discussing a fire. Fires were horrid things that destroyed lives and property, but just now she felt completely unalarmed. "That's smoke? I thought it was just a cloud."

"Yes." He straightened up.

She missed the feel of his face against her cheek. "Does it look bigger than it did before?" Her foolish heart shouted commands. *Don't leave my side so quickly. Come back. Show me. Lean close.*

"No. Thank God." He stepped down the stile. "They must be keeping it under control."

"Yes," she murmured, trying to sound pleased.

He held her hand, helped her down the old stone stairs, and led her into a vast sea of tall, still grass. Every slender stalk stood at attention, waiting for a wind to blow it, a noise to move it, an insect to bend it, but there was none. They all stood waiting.

Alex whistled, a sharp, commanding trill. She heard the sound of galloping long before the moving wraiths became distinct shapes. The grass vibrated at their coming. Three horses, shaking the earth as they ran toward them, one black as pitch and the other two fiery red blazes in the setting sun.

At least these brilliant flames she could see. They ran with tails streaming behind them, and the nearer they came, the more Willa could feel the joy with which they ran. Alex smiled like a proud parent as they galloped toward him and circled around like children eager for his attention.

The big black reared up, staving off his brothers before he trotted up to Alex, claiming his portion of attention first.

"Lord of the pasture, eh, now that Mercury is off to the races?" Alex patted the black and turned to Willa. "Allow me to introduce you to Darley's children."

The feisty stallion nudged him in the shoulder for turning away from him.

Alex responded by smoothing his hand down the big black's nose. "This ornery fellow is Midnight Streak. Midnight because that is the hour he was born, and Streak because we hope that is all one sees of him when he runs."

As if Midnight understood he was the subject under discussion, he tossed up his head and whickered.

Alex laughed. "I must warn you, his pride knows no bounds. He thinks he is the fastest and finest buck in all of England. Don't you, my boy? And perhaps he is." Alex pushed on Midnight's nose, backing him away from Willa and returning him to his brothers.

Alex brushed his fingers through the red mane of the larger of the two chestnuts. "This handsome lad is Fire Star. He's only two years old, but he'll soon be putting old Midnight through his paces, won't you, lad? There's a small star here on his nose." Alex ran his fingers lovingly over the slender white mark. "His coat is the reddest I've ever seen. See how, in this light, he almost appears to have a halo of fire?"

Alex's voice poured out rich with caring, flowing gently over the horse, falling softly on the meadow grasses, bestirring them with his affection. Willa felt like an intruder. But then, he looked over at her. "You have the same halo." It washed over her, his husky pleasure, bathing her for one golden moment in his divine tenderness. A light breeze sent waves rippling through the grass.

Behind them, at the edge of the garden, Tommy ran toward them, shouting a breathless warning. "Sir! Sir! Come quick! She's got a red bag! I saw it."

Alex swore under his breath. He pulled Willa swiftly behind him, up and over the stile. "Forgive me. I must leave you with Tommy." And with that, he bolted toward the stables.

Willa held out her skirts and hurried after him, but she may as well have tried to keep up with Fire Star or Midnight. Alex far outdistanced her.

She slowed down and tried to catch her breath. "What's a red bag?" she asked Tommy, who had matched paces with her.

"Oooh, it's bad, that's what it is, miss. It's the wrong part coming out first. The foal will drown if we don't get it out in time. And the mare, she could bleed to death."

"No. No! We can't let—" Her sentence trailed off. She charged once more down the garden path as fast as she could, praying and running. If Darley died, or the foal, what would it do to Alex? She didn't want to think of it. There must be something they could do. "There must be!" she begged the Almighty.

14

Ride a Dying Horse to Banbury Cross

The stable was ominously quiet, except for the thumping of Tommy's boots on the bricks as he and Willa hurried down the passageway. The cats sat in the shadows outside the entrance of Darley's stall, like mourners guarding a tomb. They did not stir at Willa's coming. Even the birds in the rafters had gone elsewhere to sing.

Darley lay on her side, breathing heavily. The pressure of the foal's weight against the tired mare's belly made each labored breath sound like a groan. Alex knelt at the mare's head, soothing her. When Willa entered the box, the poor creature didn't react, but merely followed her movements with wary pain-glazed eyes.

Alex glanced up. Willa had never seen him look so grim, so soldierlike. "Get a knife, boy. A knife, or anything sharp. Hurry!"

The lad ran off to the rear of the stables and disappeared.

"Willa. Take my place." Alex summoned her in

hushed tones. "Talk to her. Rub her like this. Keep her calm."

But as soon as Alex got up and Willa moved toward Darley's head, the mare rolled her eyes back showing the whites like a beast on the verge of madness. She lifted her head and thrashed, struggling to rise, even though the effort came at a great cost. She neighed, a pitiful cry for mercy.

Willa backed away.

"It's no good." Alex raked his hand through his hair. "She doesn't know you yet."

Tommy ran in, carrying a fierce-looking blade. "Should be sharp enough, sir. We use it to cut the leather. But Goliath's Dame is foaling. I got to see to 'er. Squire will hang me by my thumbs if ought 'appens to 'er."

"Go then," Alex ordered, studying the shadows on the back wall as if they might be hiding some solution to his problem.

His gaze moved to Willa. She read his desperation. He grasped her upper arm, as if she might run away or abandon him. "I need you to help me cut open the birth sack."

Cut it? She cringed. But he needed her. She nodded, and briefly studied the haphazard pattern of the straw strewn on the floor, feeling as frightened and frantic as the mare. What she needed just now was a predictable set of lines and squares. Something she could count on and arrange logically. Next time, she would be more specific when she prayed for help.

"Good." Alex swallowed hard. "I'll keep her lying still. Stay well back from her legs. You must slit the bag when it bulges out next time. Try not to cut the foal. But the important thing is to cut all the way through the membrane. Can you do it?"

She nodded. She hoped she could.

Alex put the knife in her hand and wrapped her fingers around it. He held her hand in both of his as if he could transfer some of his strength to her, stilling the ever-so-slight tremble. He took a deep breath, looking intently into her eyes. "That's my Willa. Never afraid of anything."

He left her standing there, the blade weighing heavy in her fist. He knelt beside Darley's head, blocking the horse's view of her would-be surgeon.

Willa's lips moved in a silent plea to her Maker as she edged against the rough walls of the stall toward Darley's tail. *But, I* am *afraid, she thought.*

Alex stroked Darley's neck. "That's my brave lass." Willa wasn't sure if he meant her or the horse.

"Go gently," he coaxed. "Now, wait for it to swell out. The front hooves may be inside it. Try to cut between them." His voice was low, soothing. "That's it."

Willa's heart banged so hard against her chest, if the mare did kick her, she doubted she would feel it. Her hand shook crazily as she extended the knife and waited, waited for the crimson pouch to puff out toward her.

Darley snorted, a doleful rumble that did not give rise to hope. Willa knew what was coming. The velvety red bag of veins and fluid swelled out.

"Do it, Willa." He kept his voice even and soft, but the urgency was unmistakable. "Do it now."

She pressed the knife against the bloody sack. The blade slid off to the side without making a mark. "It's slippery. I can't—"

"Use the point. Please, my love. Do it. You must or she'll die."

Willa plunged the knifepoint into the bag. Blood oozed down the steel and onto the wooden handle. She pushed it in further. Water squirted out, cleaning the knife and gushing over Willa's hand. She pulled the blade downward, slitting the bag further. Then she saw them, two sodden legs pushing their way out of the darkness. "The hooves. I can see the hooves!"

"You've done it. Oh, my sweet, you've done it." Alex shoulders relaxed.

She'd done it. The broken joy in his voice allowed the tension in her own shoulders to dissipate.

Alex leaned over and kissed Darley's cheek and patted her neck. "You're going to be fine, old girl. Fine."

In answer, Darley grunted unappreciatively.

Willa returned her attention to the miracle unfolding in front of her. "Oh! Oh my. A nose." She forgot to keep her voice low. She corrected it to an excited whisper. "Alex, I see a nose."

She beamed at him and didn't give a thought to the tear leaking down her cheek. It was all too marvelous to bother over the awkwardness of tears. Darley almost died and now—now here was a new life.

The foal came out in surges. Its head appeared partially hooded in the red sack and a blue gray skin. Willa scooted back to make way for the emerging horse.

"Make sure his nose is clear." Alex strained to see, while still pacifying Darley. "Check the nostrils."

Willa gently touched the warm, wet muzzle. "It's as clear as old Euripides's nose ever was." She smiled happily. "That's a good sign, isn't it?"

"Yes. Unless your ornery old mule always had a cabbage stuffed up his nose."

"Cabbage for brains. But not in his nose." Willa watched, mesmerized, as more and more of the baby escaped from the stretched-out opening.

It seemed impossible that from such a small dark place a whole horse should appear. Yet, here was a nose, followed by knees and a head. Then, the shoulders and the entire front legs shuddered out. Darley snorted again, this time with more energy. The rest of the foal's body gushed out onto the stable floor.

The tiny horse lay on the straw, heaving in and out as it tried to breathe. Exhausted, but alive.

It was a miracle. Willa choked back an unbidden urge to cry. She pressed her hand over her mouth lest she frighten the mare by sobbing like a silly girl who couldn't contain the wonder of it all.

Alex twisted around to see her. "Are you hurt? Did you get cut?"

She shook her head, but her watering eyes betrayed her resolve to remain stoic.

Darley lifted her head, struggling to see her new foal.

Alex went to Willa's side. He opened her fingers, still gripping the knife, and took it from her hand.

"Are you certain you are all right?" He led her to the doorway of the stall and took down an oil lantern hanging in the hall, and turned it brighter. "There's blood on your arm." He pulled out his handkerchief and was about to clean it away.

She shook her head, stopping him. "Not my blood." Her voice broke. The weight of awe was so great she might have fallen to her knees and sobbed like a baby, but for his hand supporting her arm. She gestured at the brave mare struggling to her feet. "It's hers."

Darley had made the sacrifice of all females down through the ages, the sacrifice Willa's own mother had made. She risked death to bring forth life.

Teardrops coursed down Willa's face. But she did

not wipe them away. They were good tears. She felt proud to lay claim to her gender. Perhaps men had life easier, but they would never know this. They would never walk the shadowlands of pain and death to be part of the miracle of life.

Salty water fell in straight, unfettered lines down her cheeks, blurring her vision and spotting her spectacles. She did not try to stop it. She dared not close off any part of this amazing experience, for this might be as close as she would ever come to it.

Alex turned down the lantern and hung it back on the hook. He put his arm around Willa's shoulders as they watched Darley's noble attempt to rise. At last, the new mother made it up on all fours.

Willa took off her cloudy glasses and squinted, but the fuzzy images were not any clearer. She tried to wipe her lenses on the coarse brown muslin of Alfreda's walking dress, but it only succeeded in smearing the surfaces even more. Alex silently handed her his handkerchief.

The foal lay in a heap on the straw, still breathing heavily. Darley nudged it with her nose and stood next to it, waiting. The back half of the baby horse remained shrouded in the blue-gray membrane of its former cocoon.

"Should we remove the rest of the sack?"

He shook his head, more solemn than he ought to be.

The baby was alive. Darley would live. Willa hadn't cut the foal with the knife. Everything had turned out wonderful, hadn't it? Then why did he look like a man waiting for the gallows?

Willa pushed the matter. "Perhaps we should. Only see how the little thing is stuck in it. It's exceptionally slippery. Alex?"

He didn't look at her. "If the foal doesn't get up soon, it will die."

"Let's help it up then. Surely—"

"No. It has to do it on its own. We can cover it with a blanket after she licks it. But that's all. We can't interfere."

"Stuff and nonsense! I won't stand here and watch that baby die."

"Then, you may go to the house. If there were any other way I would do it. Nature cannot be circumvented in this matter."

He would banish her to the house? She crossed her arms. How could he? She'd acted as midwife to this foal. It was her right to protect it. "I'm not feeling very fond of nature just now," she muttered.

But neither did she wish to be relegated to sitting in the kitchen of Squire Harley's house.

"Nature can be cruel." He said it under his breath, barely a whisper, a husky murmur heavily laden with resignation and pain.

She exhaled and all the fight left her.

He folded his arms protectively across his chest and then thought better of it. "When you and I were children, it robbed us of our mothers. Sometimes—" He pressed his lips together and worked his jaw before turning to her. He cupped her chin and raised it so that she met his gaze. "Sometimes, it robs mothers of their children."

Willa's hands dropped uselessly at her side. She leaned her forehead against his shoulder for comfort, and he enfolded her in his arms. They stood in the shadowed corridor, holding one another. Wordlessly, Willa listened to the slow, sad pumping of his heart. A lone drum, beating a steady sober knell, as time marched them toward Nature's verdict.

Darley snorted noisily. Alex and Willa turned to watch, holding their breath as the mother sniffed at her newborn and swiped her tongue over its nose. She pawed at the sack, stamping on it, pulling it away. The foal kicked. It was a little thing at first, but then its sticklike legs flailed against the remaining bag, tearing more of it away. Darley licked her baby again, on the face, on the neck, on the scraggly tuft at the top of its head. It was enough encouragement to make the foal scissor its legs and kick off the rest of the membrane.

"Look. A filly!" Alex exclaimed. "Darley has a daughter. Her first."

Willa smiled reservedly and nodded. No more foolish sentimentality for her. No more welling up over a life that might be snatched away in the next moment.

Darley, however, did not hold back. She sniffed and prodded at her youngster, bathing it with her tongue.

"Back away, Darley girl. Let her get up, first." Alex cautioned.

Darley tossed her head as if she understood. But of course she couldn't. Willa frowned. Darley was a beast, simply doing what any mother would do. She was like Willa. If she could, Darley would pick up the filly and set her on her feet. And *Nature* might jolly well take a flying leap off the nearest cliff. An unreasonable curse, Willa supposed. But this was not a day for reason and feasibility.

Alex gripped Willa's shoulders as he leaned forward. "Come on, little one. Get up."

The filly rocked and flailed at the air. At last, she got one front hoof planted on the floor. Her knobby knee wobbled in the air as she strained to lift her head higher. She clumsily shifted her weight and propped another hoof under her.

Alex grinned and patted Willa's arm.

He was risking hope. It worried Willa. Wasn't it better to wait and see? But how could one not hope? One look at the valiant little filly and Willa's heart was done for. The ungainly thing was all knobs and sticks, with big brown eyes, surprisingly long feminine lashes, and funny ears that pointed straight out to each side. Her coat was a lighter red than her mother's, with a broad white stripe down her nose and dainty white socks on all of her legs that only went as high as the fetlocks.

Willa clasped her hands together, twisting them, wringing them, until she couldn't contain herself any longer. She brought them up under her chin like a small child at prayer. "She's the most beautiful thing I've ever seen."

Alex looked at Willa as though she was feverish. "That?" He pointed at the filly, whose rump was now stuck up higher in the air than its head.

Her hands fell apart and she frowned at him. "Yes! And don't you dare say otherwise."

He chuckled. "In a few weeks, perhaps, when she fills out. But now?"

Her warning glare silenced his next comment, but it did nothing to dim the mocking glimmer in his eyes.

"Oh very well." He attempted to look properly chastened. "She's quite the loveliest—oh heavens, Willa, just look at her."

The poor thing had one hind leg standing upright, but the angle of it forced her chest to the ground, so that she looked more like a large malformed spider than a horse.

Oblivious of his criticism, Darley whickered, approving of her daughter's efforts.

"Oh, Alex, can't we help her?"

"No. Just wait. She's nearly got it." His arm slipped to Willa's waist, and he gave her a friendly hug. "Patience, my dear."

My dear? He shouldn't use endearments so freely. They might confuse other women. Naturally, Willa knew better. It was just his way, warm and charming. All rakes and rogues were able to make women feel like giddy schoolgirls, were they not? It stood to reason. Fortunately, Willa did not succumb so easily to casual endearments.

The filly managed to slide another rear leg into the upright position. Darley whickered happily. And Alex chuckled.

With Herculean effort the little filly pushed up on her front legs, but collapsed in a tangled pile.

"Oh no," Willa moaned.

"Not to worry. She's got it now. Just went at it wrong. This time she'll do it right. Front first. Back second. It often takes four or five tries." Alex pulled Willa with him to the support post at the opening of the stall and leaned against it, holding her next to him as they watched.

Willa felt him kiss the top of her head before he rested his chin on her wayward pile of curls. One small kiss, but it melted away all the tension in her body. One insignificant friendly kiss, no matter how much she might wish otherwise.

"You're relieved, aren't you?" It was a silly thing to say. Of course, he was. What she really meant was, *That's why you kissed me, isn't it? You're happy.*

He didn't answer with words. It was a low murmur of agreement and a tightening of his hold on her.

Hush, Willa, she scolded herself, *this is not a day for analyzing.* It was a day long past ordinary logic and rational behavior, a day to simply enjoy. She nestled happily against him to watch the newborn flop and twist in an attempt to stand.

Ultimately, Alex was right. On the fourth try, the filly pushed up with her front legs, and her hindquarters followed suit. Although her legs bowed out alarmingly, as if the joints weren't precisely certain which direction to bend, the foal finally stood on all fours.

"Now will she live?"

He nodded. "If she can find her mother's teat, her chances are good."

Darley licked her daughter, every stroke of her tongue claiming ownership of her offspring.

"What will you name her?" she whispered.

Alex straightened and turned her towards him. It pleased her that he kept his arms tucked securely around her. "I believe that honor should fall to you. After all, you were her midwife."

Willa leaned back in his embrace. "But, she's your horse. I couldn't."

"She would not be alive without your help." He smiled warmly at Willa. Her harebrained heart began to dance a wild jig.

He tucked back one of her curls, skimming her cheek with his fingertips. "Well? What will you choose?"

Her thoughts turned to gibberish, and her breath snagged, making her gulp before she could speak. "Choose?" Choose what? Him? Yes. Done. But, of course, that wasn't the question. "What was the question again?"

"What name." The rascal grinned.

She didn't know where her cockles were located, nor *what* they were, but she was fairly certain they were warming nicely. Instead of properly organized rational speech, her words flowed out in a nervous rush, a high-pitched embarrassing vomit, splashing across his shirtfront. "My favorite name is Sally. It sounds so bright and cheerful. I've always wanted to name something Sally. But Jerome insisted all of our animals must have Greek names. Greek *poets* to be exact. Even the cats, Sophocles and Hesiod. Our parakeet was Homer. But he died. So, yes, I would very much like to name her Sally."

"Ah, yes." He nodded patiently, sagely. "Sally, now there's a name to strike terror in the heart of the other racehorses."

"Oh." She smiled sheepishly at his jibe. "Well, we might call her Valiant Sally. That's a little better, don't you think?"

"Valiant, yes?" He studied Willa's face as if her lips and eyes held a secret list of names. "Valiant Sal."

She swallowed, uneasy under the warmth of his gaze. "Yes. Valiant Sal. That sounds quite wonderful."

"Not unlike my Valiant Willa."

He leaned closer, his mouth only a breath away from hers. And Willa would have fallen gladly into his tantalizing kiss had she not desperately required the truth of the matter. "Am I? Yours? *Your* Willa?"

Her question startled him. If she could have swallowed the words back she would. But it was too late. She'd aroused him from their dream.

He let go of her. And that was far more answer than she wanted.

In the distance, she heard the clattering of wheels on the cobblestones and the sound of men's voices out in the yard. The squire and his servants were back.

She stepped away from him.

15

A Diller, a Dollar a Ten O'clock Scholar

Tommy bolted out of a stall and ran headlong down the passageway to greet the master with good news. "Goliath's Dame, she's about to foal! Come an' see."

A group of weary men followed the lad up the hall. Slapping one another good-naturedly, their triumphant voices and feet filled the quiet stable with joviality.

Squire Harley called out to Alex. "We got the fire put down, right as rain."

"Could've used some rain." The man next to him wiped some of the soot from his brow onto his sleeve.

"Aye. That we could've. The barn and his north field burned to the ground. Ridley is done in. Says he wants out. Too old to manage the place. Wants to take the waters in Bath. Phah! Stay on the land, says I. But, no, says he, sell the place for a song if anyone's willing to sing.

"But what's this?" He slapped Alex on the shoulder. "Darley's foal nursing already? And where are my manners?" He bowed to Willa. "You must excuse me, miss. It's been a day better left untallied."

Alex introduced her as his cousin. A prevarication she didn't bother to correct. The good squire offered the loan of his dogcart and groom so that Alex might convey them both back to London, then trudged off to await the newest member of his stable.

The ride home was silent, but not quiet, for certainly Willa heard the groom humming in the rear seat, the rhythm of the wheels clacking against the road, the steady tattoo of the horse's gait, crickets sawing their two-note tune, the whistling skree of hawks as they wheeled in the night sky, hunting mice in the field, but most of all she heard breathing. This was not the in-and-out, unconscious drawing of air. Alex's breathing was devoid of rhythm, full of hesitation, stops and starts, deep and shallow. She knew it to be the sound of a man thinking, the uneasy cadence of a man ruminating, lamenting, brooding, and in the end reflecting.

Odd, that his unsettled breathing should put her at ease. Her own fell into a steady contented tempo that lulled her to sleep long before they reached the noise of London. She awoke with her head resting on his shoulder and her aunt's town house looming down the street.

The next morning Willa was surprised to find her aunt sitting at her customary place at the end of the table in the breakfast room.

"Good morning, my dear. Do not look at me as if you've seen a ghost. Have some breakfast." She waved at the sideboard. "Did you pass the evening pleasantly?"

Willa felt herself blanche. "Pleasant enough. And yourself?" She picked up a plate.

"And how did you spend it?" Honore speared a strawberry and twirled her fork, showing excessive interest in the plump red heart before popping it in her mouth.

Willa took a deep breath and stilled the trembling

serving spoon in her hand. The truth. It was always better to come directly to the point. "If you must know, I helped a horse give birth. Most diverting, but I should probably spare you the details as they are decidedly not conducive to good digestion."

"Worried about my digestion, eh?" Honore pulled apart a small blueberry muffin and liberally buttered one half. "How thoughtful. And young Braeburn?"

"Kind enough to bring me home." Willa filled her plate and sat down. "Nothing more, if that is what you are thinking."

Honore's face turned glum. "How dull." She bit into the muffin and chewed thoughtfully.

Willa shrugged and stared at her food with mounting disinterest.

Honore licked the butter from her lips. "No matter. On the morrow Tournsby promised to collect us for the races? That should be a diverting afternoon."

"The races? I should think not. When last I saw Lord Tournsby he was nearly dead." Willa shoved a sausage to the far side of her plate. "It will be several weeks before he's fit enough to be moved from Lady Tricot's house."

"Are you quite certain? In my experience, gentlemen usually recover from their little escapades with more alacrity than that."

"Quite certain. Nearly dead." Willa stabbed her kipper and sawed it apart vigorously. *Nearly dead.* And the blame lay squarely on her shoulders.

"Hhmm." Honore shrugged. "The silly nodcock. Plunging himself into the Thames."

Willa frowned. "You know why he did it, don't you?"

"I have my suspicions. Willa, dearest, do stop mutilating that poor fish."

It was time to beard the lion in her den, or pull the

cat's whiskers, or do whatever she must to make her aunt squash the problematic rumor she'd set into motion.

Willa plunked her knife down on the tablecloth beside her plate. "You must tell everyone the truth. I insist upon it."

"The truth?"

"Yes. You know perfectly well, you have no intention of making me your heir."

"Oh, I don't know." Honore flicked her palm out as if it were of no consequence. "Has to go to someone. Why not you?"

Willa crossed her arms and glared at her aunt skeptically. "You're using it as bait. A scent to stir up the hounds. A trick, to make the hunt more entertaining."

Honore smacked her hand on the breakfast table, rattling the dishes. "I can't imagine where everyone gets such wicked notions about me!" She narrowed her eyes at Willa, gauging her prey like a lioness stalking a very slow lummox.

Willa swallowed. *The bearding was not going well.*

Honore raised her voice, emphasizing the depth of her invisible injury. "You're beginning to sound exactly like your cousin Fiona. It's as if all of you think I'm capable of horridly elaborate machinations. Monstrous! You must think I'm some sort of devious Prince Michelangelo."

Willa blinked. Perhaps she'd heard wrong. "Do you mean, Machiavelli?"

"You see?" Honore held out her hand, beseeching Willa. "I don't even know the fellow's name. How simple I am? Your accusations wound me to my very soul." She clapped a hand over her bosom.

Doing it up a bit brown, Willa thought. But to her astonishment, Honore actually developed moisture in her eyes, as if she were truly on the verge of tears. Willa stared at her for a moment before bursting into laughter.

"I may be nearly blind, but I'm not daft." She rushed to her aunt's chair and knelt beside her. "*Simple?* You? Never! If I've wounded you, I apologize. You're a remarkable woman, Aunt Honore. Brilliant! But, yes, it's true. I do believe you are capable of elaborate schemes. And perhaps some rather ingenious mischief. The more complex the plot, the happier you are. Am I wrong?"

Honore sniffed. "Oh pooh. Now, you're just flattering me."

Willa laughed. "Only you would think it."

Honore sat back in her chair, regarding Willa as a gardener evaluates a rose. Is it too soon to cut her from the bush, or too late? Crush the blossom? Or save the flower? What was her aunt thinking?

Honore folded her arms across her chest and nodded. "I quite like you."

Willa smiled.

"For pity sake, get up from the floor. You'll bruise your knees."

"You'll call off the hounds?"

Honore arched one eyebrow. "What would you have me do, send a notice to the *Times*? 'To whom it may concern, my niece is very nearly a pauper. Take warning one and all. She has naught but a pittance for a dowry, and no other expectations whatsoever.' Is that what you have in mind?"

Willa stood up and fidgeted with her skirt. "Something a trifle less humiliating."

"Oh, it's humiliation you wish to avoid?"

"I wish to avoid fortune hunters who want to sink

rowboats so that they might appear as my knight in shining armor."

Honore shrugged and smeared marmalade on a piece of toast. "More entertaining than cards or the juggler, wouldn't you say?"

"Yes, but infinitely more dangerous."

"I quite enjoyed watching your beau gallop around the pond to save the roly-poly chap."

"Precisely my point, Harry might have died."

"Fiddle-faddle. Your Alex is quite athletic. Never a question."

"He's not *my* Alex. You are diverting from the point. Something must be done about the fortune hunters."

Honore held up her toast, waving it like wand. "Aside from humiliating you in the *Times* or the *Post*, I'm at a loss."

"I should think a few well-placed words, in the right ear, might do the trick."

Honore's expression grew shrewd. "Been known to backfire. Ofttimes, a denial is far more convincing than a declaration."

Willa's shoulders sagged. What chance did she have of convincing Honore to do the proper thing?

The butler entered, carrying a silver salver bearing a card. He spoke in hushed tones to Honore, who chuckled. "Yes. Yes, by all means, send them in."

Her aunt grinned at her. "Delightful news, my dear. Your brother has come to call."

"Jerome?"

"You have another brother?"

"Of course not."

"Well then, it must be he. Cairn tells me, there is a bee under the good vicar's bonnet. Ah, here he is. Let us see this bee." Honore dropped her toast and rubbed her hands together like an eager child on Christmas morn.

In the next instant, her features reverted to the very epitome of a bored matron. Willa adjusted her spectacles and squinted, looking for a residue of the excitement previously flashing in her aunt's features. Nothing. *Extraordinary.*

Jerome charged into the breakfast room, waving a parchment as if it were a battle flag. "I've had a letter. Most alarming."

Sir Daniel trailed behind him and cleared his throat. "To be precise, the letter was mine."

"Oh, yes, to be sure. So it was." Jerome sputtered and inclined his head. "Sir Daniel has had a letter of alarming proportions."

"Looks to be of normal proportions to me." Honore glanced at him quizzically.

"Not what I meant."

"No? What did you mean?"

"Upsetting, that's what! Can't tolerate this sort of thing. Must take Willa home, forthwith and immediately."

"Forthwith? *And* immediately? Come, nephew, what can you be talking about?"

Jerome shook the letter. "Gossip, that's what. A warning. Rackety crowd, it says." Jerome skimmed the letter, searching for the right words. He jabbed his finger at the handwriting in the center. "Right here. Says, you abandoned her. Left her at the mercy of young Braeburn and the like. Spreading rumors about her money."

He dropped his arms to his side and took a deep breath. "Can't have that."

"No," Honore agreed, calmly stirring her hot

chocolate. "Especially dangerous, the hum about her money, since she doesn't have any. Unless, you . . . ?"

"No." Jerome raised his hands, warding her off, still clutching the "letter of alarming proportions." "No. Not my point, at all. Don't care about the money. It's the rackety crowd business. And leaving Willa to the devices of a wastrel like Braeburn. Can't be entrusted to the likes of him. Who knows what he—"

"No! Alex would never . . ." Willa swallowed back the rest of her sentence. She clenched her hands into tight fists, forcing the nails to bite into her palms so that she might gain control and calm her voice to a respectable level. "Jerome, I beg you. Do not say such things of him. You mustn't call him names or slur his character. It's not true. He's not a wastrel. What do either of you know of him?"

Sir Daniel patted her on the shoulder. "Now, now, Willa. He is my brother, you know. I know whereof I speak."

She moved out from under his grasp. "You turned your back on him long ago. He's no longer a confused boy. If you would but look, he's—"

"Yes. Yes." Honore held up her hand. "My dear, before you wax eloquent on young Braeburn's character, I should like to ask your brother who was the author of this *alarming letter*?"

Jerome shrank back and colored slightly.

"Well?" Honore narrowed her eyes at him as she sipped her morning chocolate.

He shook his head and muttered to the floor. "Anonymous."

"What?" She turned her ear toward him. "Didn't quite hear what you said."

"That's the rub, you see. No signature. No address. Anonymous."

Sir Daniel nodded. "One of my acquaintances, to be sure. Well-meaning, no doubt. Trying to be of assistance."

"Ah. Anonymous." Honore stood up and shook the crumbs from her silk skirt. "And the postmark? Could it have been posted from Essex?"

Sir Daniel and Jerome took a step closer to each other. Daniel rubbed at his knuckles. "Why, yes. I believe it may have been."

"As I thought." She turned to Willa. "Congratulations, my dear. You must have made Miss Tricot so jealous that she has gone to these extraordinary lengths to have you removed from her sphere."

"Oh, but I cannot think that Alfreda would write—"

"Tut tut, Willa. Think, child. Is it not posted from her neighborhood? You mustn't underestimate your confederates. She's a very determined female, is she not? And is not Lord Tournsby hanging about you like a puppy dog?"

"Hardly that! But how did you know she . . ." There was no way to continue the question without divulging Alfreda's secret goal.

One side of Honore's face cocked up in a devious grin. "I make a point of—"

"Here now. What's this?" Jerome interrupted. "There's a lord paying heed to our Willa?"

Honore wheeled around. "Why, yes, there is. Mind you, I won't have any of it. He's not nearly good enough for our Willa."

"Not good enough? A gentleman with a title? Surely—"

Honore waved her hand glibly. "No. Not good enough by half."

Jerome rubbed his chin. "Well, I had thought to take her home with us, but—"

"What?" Honore puffed up like a dragon, towering over poor Jerome. "You thought you'd barge in here and whisk her away simply because she's garnered a jealous enemy? Are you daft?"

Willa felt sorry for her brother as Honore completely turned the tables on him. He'd come on Willa's behalf, and Honore was eating him alive.

Willa didn't wish to leave. Not yet. She would spend many long decades at Jerome's side in St. Cleve. This was her one chance for adventure, for stolen moments with Alex. She couldn't bear the thought of parting from him forever. Not yet. The time would come soon enough. But this one Season, these few delicious moments, would have to last her a lifetime.

Jerome and Daniel were completely baffled as Honore threw up her hands and stomped out of the room without another word.

Willa moved to her brother's side. "I assure you, Jerome, I am quite well. I'm deeply moved that you traveled to Town to come to my aid. I am most grateful. But as you can see I am fine. You know me to be a sensible person, do you not?"

He nodded, somewhat mollified.

"I promise you I shall write immediately should the circumstances get out of hand. But, for the nonce, I would very much like to stay with our aunt."

He sputtered. "Yes. Yes. Had no idea you had *lords* hanging about. Never would have guessed it." He shook his head. "Quite remarkable." He tucked the letter away in his pocket. "And, Willa, if Aunt Honore puts any of the gentlemen off too quickly, you could always have them apply to me. A lord is nothing to turn up your nose at."

She hugged him. "You are the best of brothers."

He blushed and patted her arms. "I trust you will use your good judgment."

Sir Daniel stood stiffly beside Jerome. "Yes, in *all* matters. Be wary. Write us at the slightest hint of trouble."

Jerome nodded. "Now, I expect you had better go make our apologies before she overboils and sends you home herself. We'll see ourselves out."

Willa hurried up the staircase to find her aunt seated behind her escritoire in her sitting room, placidly writing a note.

"I take it Jerome relented?" Honore asked without looking up.

"You *knew* he would."

Honore shrugged.

Willa squinted at Honore, gauging each nuance of her aunt's supposed nonchalance. "I wonder who wrote that letter, for I am convinced Alfreda would not have done." Willa listened carefully for any changes in her aunt's breathing.

"No, probably not."

"But? You suggested that she—"

"You wished to stay here, did you not?" Honore chuckled and shook her head as if Willa were a foolish child. She glanced up. "Perhaps Alex wrote the letter."

"Alex? No, that's ridiculous. What possible motive would he have?"

"Ah, you want motive, do you?" Honore brushed the end of her feather quill against her cheek as she gazed speculatively at Willa. "He might wish to protect you from his baser nature?"

"No. I don't believe it." Willa crossed her arms firmly across her chest.

Honore's eyebrows rose theatrically. "What is it you don't believe? That he has a baser nature? Or that he would wish to protect you from it?"

"Neither one." She was adamant.

As her aunt's lips curled sideways in a private joke, Willa realized her error. "No, that's not what I meant. He doesn't have a base nature and of course he would protect me from it."

"Naturally." Honore's amused expression remained intact. "If he had one—"

"You know perfectly well what I meant." She flung her hands to her side and inhaled deeply before trying to breach any more of her aunt's verbal traps. "He did not write it." She put a staccatolike emphasis on each word.

Honore tipped her head to the side and studied Willa. "Very well. Then, who?"

Willa frowned and leaned forward, placing both hands squarely on her aunt's writing table. "Were I able to discern any rational motive, I would think it was you."

"I?" She drew back, hand to heart, offended but amused all at the same time. "Me? Why I've done nothing wrong, except dote on you to excess. The excitement yesterday must have gone to your head. Go have a lie down. Tell that badger of a lady's maid to bring you something to soothe your feverish mind. Laudanum, for instance." Honore chuckled a little too giddily as she waved Willa away. She continued to complain as Willa obediently turned to go. "I? Indeed. And whyever would I do such a thing?"

Willa frowned. *Why, indeed?*

16

The Queen of Hearts She Spied Some Tarts All on a Summer's Eve

The following evening, Willa walked down the hallway to her aunt's study. It startled her when the door opened before she reached it. A man slipped out of the room quickly, efficiently, his boots scarcely making a sound on the marble.

She'd seen him before, coming and going secretly, like a rat-catcher no one wishes to acknowledge. His long coat was marred with dried mud and bore the dirt of weeks of hard wear without benefit of a proper brushing. He frowned at Willa, eyes shrewd and ferret-like, assessing in a glance, seeing more than one wished. He did not bow. Did naught but place his hat on his head and tip it slightly in deference to her approach, before he hurried away.

Willa frowned as he disappeared down the back stairs. She quietly entered the room he'd just vacated. "Who was that?"

Honore looked up from her escritoire. "Who, dear?"

She knew by her aunt's initial response there would

be no answer; nevertheless, Willa tried to extract more. "The very odd man who was just in here. The man wearing a coat, when it is not in the least bit chilly outside."

Honore's brows pinched together as if she were trying to recollect one particular visitor from a collection of hundreds that had just evacuated her study. "Men wear coats for many reasons and in all seasons. My dear! You look stunning in that gown. The dark blue silk is exactly the right shade to complement your hair. I knew it would be. Come. I have a sapphire necklace that will match it perfectly."

The necklace was beautiful. Unfortunately, it dangled, much to Willa's embarrassment, into the cleft between her breasts. If, perchance, a gentleman failed to notice the ample expanse of her bosom revealed by the gown's wide, square neckline, an arrow of dazzling blue gems would point his gaze where it should not go.

Willa shook her head. "Thank you, but I couldn't. It's lovely, but . . ." *What phrase would extricate her from the vulgarity of the jeweled collar?* "I'm afraid it's too expensive . . . too magnificent a piece for a young lady of my station."

"Hhmm." Honore stood behind her, looking in the mirror, her forefinger tapping speculatively against her chin. "Yes, I see the problem. I'll adjust the clasp. Just so." She grinned, pleased with the result of her ministrations. "Yes. Now it's perfect."

Now the exquisite rope of sapphires ended with the star cluster suspended a tantalizing inch above where her breasts arced together. The pendant no longer dropped vulgarly, like a finger, into her cleavage. Instead, one must watch it shimmer and barely graze that dark place. Egad! Her aunt was a seductive genius, a sorceress.

"I ought not wear this." Willa muttered.

Her aunt simply laughed. "But you will. Now come. Let us go. We have a thousand people to visit."

A thousand people? Honore was prone to exaggeration. But in this instance, her aunt's estimate proved to be conservative.

The routs they attended were jammed with people. Indeed, they had to wait in the carriage for nearly an hour to disembark in front of each house. Then, they must push and squeeze their way up the stairs, wait endlessly in a line to parade past the matron of the home, and do a curtsy. After which, they wriggled back down the staircase, ducking under elbows, dodging cups of warm punch, and at last, they pushed their way out the front door into the night air, took a deep breath, climbed into the carriage, rode a block and a half, and proceeded to do it all over again.

Willa could not endure one more rout that night. Her aunt refused to hear her protests. Honore clucked her tongue. "Lady Haversburg will be offended if we do not go. She is all agog to meet you. Sent me the 'at home' weeks ago. We must go." She craned around to peek out the back window.

"She won't even notice if we are there." Willa rubbed at her temple.

Honore snorted. "Speak for yourself, my dear. Everyone knows when I am in attendance. I cannot be missed." Indeed, in a beaded emerald green gown contrasting her deep red-hennaed hair, Honore commanded attention.

Willa endured Lady Haversburg's ordeal. When, at last, they escaped to the carriage, she declared herself completely done in and fit company for no one but her own pillow.

"Folderol! It's only one o'clock. No one goes to bed this early. One more stop. Lady Vessmere's card party, where you may sit down to your heart's content."

"My feet are not what is sore. It's my ribs from being jabbed and shoved. Are you certain the card party won't be another button-to-eyeball crush? At Lady Haversburg's rout my hair snagged on Lord Alberney's stickpin. He dragged me backwards up two stairs before he noticed."

"Yes, well, that explains it. I thought perhaps you were adopting a rather unique new style. Come here. I will tuck it down for you."

Willa shifted across the carriage to sit beside her aunt. "Promise the card party shan't be another horrid squeeze."

"It's a charitable event. Those are never as well attended." Honore gently prodded and tucked Willa's wayward curls back into the ribbons coiling in the Greek mode through her hair.

"Charity? How lovely. Then I shall be happy to go. Is it for orphans? Stricken soldiers? Which?"

"Ah, well, nothing quite so noble I'm afraid. Turn your head, dear. This stubborn piece keeps springing out."

Willa obeyed. "All charity is noble."

"If you say so. I expect Lady Vessmere feels the same way. The late baron left her with a pile of debts and no means to pay. So, every Thursday she holds an evening of cards and entertainment. Those in attendance generally leave her a percentage of their winnings. There! Your hair is restored."

Willa returned to her seat across the carriage and frowned. "I'm not quite certain that qualifies as charity. Usually, it is for those less fortunate than ourselves."

Honore strained to see out the back window again. "I daresay she *was* less fortunate. Debtors' prison might have killed her. Gaol fever, you know."

"Oh. I see." Willa frowned, trying to harmonize her former ideas of charity with her aunt's more liberal application. When at last she decided it was a useless exercise, she noticed Honore twisting in her seat again. "Why do you keep peering out the rear window? Is something amiss? Are we being followed by brigands?"

"Brigands? Ha! Don't be absurd. Willa, really, you mustn't pinch up your face. You wouldn't want frown wrinkles at your age."

Alex wondered for the hundredth time that evening what he was doing here. He reminded himself he'd come because Harry had escaped from Tournsby's sickbed and dragged him out for the evening. At least, these stakes were not high as the moon, and Harry was not losing as much as he would have at faro.

Alex ought to be content. He sat at a table playing *vingt et un* with his friends, a brandy at his elbow, a beautiful woman leaning enticingly over his shoulder, her perfume coiling around his nostrils like a hypnotic snake. All night, the cards kept turning up in his favor. Davies was spilling over with amusing jibes, which ought to be enormously entertaining. Harry certainly found everything Davies said hilarious.

The dealer handed Alex a ten of spades. Coupled with the ten he already held, it meant, in all likelihood, he need only stand pat in order to win once again. He ought to be happy. A gambler enjoyed winning, did he not? Then why was he not jubilant?

It was as if in another game, an invisible game, he'd laid down a winning hand and lost something of infinitely greater value than the shekels riding on the table tonight. He deserved to lose here as well. If he lost a large sum at *vingt et un,* he would be justified in the doldrums he felt.

Funny how fate loves an irony. He chuckled, *not* at Davies' witty joke, but at fate's mockery.

"Devil take it," he muttered. If he felt like losing, he would. He asked for another card. It turned up the ace of hearts.

Davies whistled softly. "Devil take it, indeed. What did you do? Sell him your soul. I declare you cannot lose this evening."

Harry answered for him. "Yes, yes. Devilishly lucky chap! Bargained away his soul long ago, I should think."

Was that it? Was he soulless? Had he trifled with life so long that happiness would forever elude him? Would he be trapped in this river of emptiness for the rest of his days?

He'd chosen this life, hadn't he? Or, had it just swept him up and carried him along like the Thames had done with Harry?

The lady at his shoulder leaned close and whispered beside his ear—a piquant taunt designed to arouse the devil in him. He scarcely heard her. Instead, Alex dribbled a stack of coins into her hand and asked her to find him another brandy, as this one had been breathing for far too long.

What was he doing here?

Infernal plagued question.

He would do better to ask himself where he would rather be. Home, he decided, sleeping in his bed, or . . . in a stable? Watching Darley suckle her new foal? Yes, with Willa wrapped tightly in his arms.

That way madness lies. The bard was right. He plowed his fingers into his hair above his ear and pulled at it.

Davies arched one brow. "Come. It cannot be as disconcerting as all that to win."

Harry nodded. "Ruining your hair, old chum. Look like a madman. Supposed to be the windswept, not the hand-swept." Harry fell into gales of laughter at his own feeble joke. Fortunately, he was too far into his cups to notice that Alex was not in the least amused.

Alex was busy trying to decipher the specter standing in the doorway. Perhaps, he truly had gone mad. The vision before him looked exactly like Willa, stunningly so. Lady Vessmere replaced Alex's brandy and kissed his cheek proprietarily. He moved not a muscle for fear the apparition would evaporate.

If Willa expected to see a roomful of gentlemen with crepe tied about their arms and ladies clad in somber black dresses, playing sedate games of penny lou and whist, she was sorely mistaken.

"A house of cards," she said under her breath.

Honore prodded the doorframe with one finger. "I don't think it will fall down tonight. Stop standing with your mouth agape like a country bumpkin. Oh, look there is Lord Monmouth." She waved and left Willa standing in the doorway.

They were light-skirts. Members of the *demimonde.* Willa wasn't sure how she knew it, but she did. They didn't have kohl darkening their eyes, as she had always imagined, nor brightly painted lips. Their gowns were beautiful, and hardly more daring than the one she wore.

She could be wrong. To her left a pianist and violinist played a tasteful sonata. To her right an enormous Indian servant stood like a statue guarding the occupants. He looked precisely like one of the eunuchs drawn in her storybooks, an open black vest over a white lawn shirt with blousy sleeves and pantaloons with oriental stitching, wonderful pointed shoes, and a massive scimitar sheathed from his belt. They had to be light-skirts.

Willa squinted and formulated a theory. The men in the room outnumbered the ladies by a mere handful. A telling detail. Most social and charitable gatherings offered a plethora of females, debutantes along with their mothers or chaperones. This room held very few matrons. Aside from her aunt, there was only one other lady Willa recognized.

Another fact tipped the balance sheet. These women moved differently, subtle suggestive movements that took the unlearned observer a moment or two to comprehend. There were no demure glances to the floorboards. These women allowed their elegantly tapered fingers to rest intimately on gentlemen's arms and shoulders. Hips swayed. Fans fluttered and snapped in a variety of codes Willa knew better than to translate. The laughter was flirtatious, belying the restrained decorum of the music.

Charity? Ha! This was no better than a gaming hell. One brazen woman leaned forward to hand a man a brandy snifter, her bosom lowered for his view a long, indecent moment. When he failed to take proper notice she wantonly kissed him on the cheek. In public!

Alex! Willa inhaled sharply and hid her mouth behind her hand. It was Alex, as astonished to see Willa as she was to see him. Alex. With that trollop purring in his ear.

Willa had to think. But *he* was staring at her. Thoughts whooshed through her head like hysterical bats disturbed in the daytime.

She had an urge to grab the eunuch's fearsome sword and order that promiscuous hussy to whisper her poison elsewhere. She envisioned herself standing on a table, waving the mighty blade like Joan of Arc and ordering them to all go home and behave themselves like proper gentlemen and ladies.

A sermon! How she would like to deliver them all a scorching sermon.

They would laugh.

Willa seized a shallow breath. She could flee, run out of the room, down the stairway, and out into the night, where blackness would enfold her in a blind fog. Perhaps that was her only course. Run away.

She turned to go and collided with Lord Alberney's stickpin for the second time that evening.

He gave her a friendly pat on the shoulders. "Here now. What's this? Going so soon? What's your hurry, my beauty? Don't believe I've had the pleasure." He bowed.

She wanted, nay, she needed to scold someone. Lord Alberney had crossed paths with the wrong woman. "Oh we've met, my lord. Don't tell me you don't remember dragging me upstairs at Lady Haversburg's."

He laughed raucously. "Dragged you upstairs, did I?" He squinted at her, trying to recall. "Deuced pretty if it weren't for those thick lenses. A pity I don't remember. Must've been completely foxed to forget a night like that. Never mind. Come. Sit with me." He put an arm around her waist and whispered loudly, breath laced with the biting tang of whiskey. "P'rhaps we can have a rematch, eh?"

Fire rushed up her neck and burst into her cheeks as she realized how he'd misconstrued her meaning. She pushed at his voluminous chest and tried to wriggle out of his grasp. "No, my lord. I fear you've completely misunderstood—"

Another hand grasped her firmly around the middle and pulled her free of Lord Alberney's arm.

She knew that hand, the size, the feel of it around her, heard the growl rumbling in his chest, and knew without question who it was.

Alex's voice was low, carefully punctuated to sound genial, but nonetheless threatening. "There must be some mistake, my lord. The young lady is with me."

Lord Alberney snorted derisively, and muttered to himself, before answering, "Don't' see how. Practically threw herself into m'arms."

Alex tightened his grip on her. "Lost your way, did you, my dear?"

Willa, sandwiched in the close space between the two large men, looked up at him and frowned. "Not as badly as you have."

17

A Peck of Pickled Peppers

Alex pulled Willa past Lord Alberney, out into the vestibule. He held her by both shoulders and spoke in a whisper that managed to sound like a shout. "What in heaven's name are you doing here?"

She clamped her lips shut. He didn't deserve a response, not unless she gave him the scathing set-down brewing in her head, the one unfit to be delivered in public. "Who was that woman?"

He held her shoulders, staring into her face. "What woman?"

She glared at him. "I'm not completely blind. You know perfectly well which woman. That woman."

He turned his head to the side, following the direction in which she frowned.

The woman in question stood in the doorway watching them, an annoyingly well-formed creature who managed to wear violet to advantage, though why she bothered with the black lace trim Willa could not imagine, hardly a suitable mourning gown.

Alex turned back to Willa. "Lady Vessmere?"

Willa exhaled loudly and muttered, "I ought to have known."

At the sound of her name the woman drew near. "What is it, Alex? You left the table so abruptly."

He straightened and turned, blocking Willa from Lady Vessmere's view. "Nothing. A family matter. My cousin. In need of assistance."

Willa peeked around him, fixing the widow with the most imperious stare she could manage.

Lady Vessmere smiled cunningly. "Your cousin?" She gracefully floated to the right, peering at Willa with undisguised interest. "I was under the impression this young lady arrived with Lady Alameda?"

Alex continued to try to shield Willa from his hostess's prying eyes. "If you would be so kind as to make my excuses to Harry. I must escort my young cousin home."

Willa and Lady Vessmere edged out from behind his inadequate screen to evaluate one another.

Alex deepened his timbre into one that brooked no argument. "It is a matter of some importance."

The lady cocked her head slightly, appearing to acquiesce. "As you wish. Shall I also inform Lady Alameda that her niece will be leaving with you? She is the lady's niece, is she not?"

Alex stepped back, his jaw muscles flexing. He glared at them both. "No. I shall tell her myself." He gruffly abandoned them in the foyer and went to her aunt's table.

Willa crossed her arms, waiting impatiently.

"Intriguing." The merry widow inspected Willa as though she were a prize pig at the fair. "You're not the sort I thought he would succumb to."

Willa held her chin aloft and tried, in vain, to arch one brow like her aunt could do. Instead, both brows went up. "I have no idea what you are talking about. However, I do know this is no charity gathering you are hosting. You make a mockery of real charities that would benefit orphans or the wounded from our battlefields."

"A charity? Gad! Is that what she told you?" Lady Vessmere put her fingers to her mouth and giggled with undisguised glee. "How very diverting."

Willa suddenly felt like a cake. A gigantic, green, crumbling cake.

She averted her eyes, glancing into the card room. Her aunt was conducting an animated argument without looking up from her cards, and then she shooed Alex away as if he were an annoyance.

When he returned to the foyer, Lady Vessmere was still chuckling. "She's charming, Alex. Most amusing." The wretched woman grinned wickedly, trailing her fingers across his shoulder, and twittering one last time before returning to her guests. "I bid you a pleasant evening."

Willa rushed away, practically running down the staircase.

They had all betrayed her.

Alex followed loudly on the stairs behind her, but she reached the entry ahead of him. Another Indian servant bowed before her and opened the front door.

She hurried out into the darkness, grateful for its cloak. Lanterns hissed and flickered on the carriages along the street, but surely those pinpricks could not illuminate her humiliation fully. She quickened her step.

The tattoo of his shoes on the walk closed in on her. He grabbed her arm, clasping it firmly. She knew there was no hope of escape.

"Where do you think you are going?" He sounded

harsh. Foreign. He was not her Alex. Not the one who had cooed soothingly to Darley. Not the Alex she knew, easy and relaxed, ready with a tease. Hard Alex. "Do you even know where you are? This is not Mayfair. A block or two in that direction would put you in the midst of some very interesting company." He gave her arm a tug. "Well?"

Where was she going?

Willa had been quizzed all her life. Answers came readily to her. But this time, she realized, she had no answer. She was running away. That was all. Simple. Irrational. Fraught with complicating factors; nevertheless, that was it.

"Away!" She glared up at him, defying him to challenge her conclusion.

He stared back at her, obviously unmoved by her wrath.

Away, where? He might ask, and she would have to say, *I don't know. Away from you.* But saying so would tell him far too much, far more than she was willing to tell.

He seemed to be doing some lengthy calculations of his own. She grew uneasy under his scrutiny.

"Very well. Then I will take you there."

He kept hold of her arm while signaling for a hack. Grumbling under his breath until one obliged him and stopped. He jerked open the door, saving the coachman the bother, and maneuvered Willa up the steps into the sultry confines of the conveyance.

18

Duck, Duck, Goose!

"I suppose you think I am grateful."

"Nothing of the kind."

"Good." Willa crossed her arms and settled back against the worn leather squibs. The coach windows were smudged and a smattering of soot and dirt made it nearly impossible for her to distinguish anything out in the darkness. She sat in deliberate sulky silence. She had no reason to speak to him. No reason at all. Save one small matter. "Where are we going?"

Alex sat across from her, studying her with the haughty disdain of a perturbed parent. The push and pull of the old coach made his broad shoulders sway from side to side. He took his time before answering. "I gave him your aunt's direction."

"I don't want to go there either." She cocked her head to the left, chin held high.

He answered more quickly this time and with a modicum of compassion in his tone. "I can't blame you. The woman is a lunatic. Where then?" His forbearance was short-lived. He didn't let the moment pass without adding a mocking bite. "*Away?*"

She clamped her lips together. "She's not a lunatic."

Alex exhaled loudly. "Oh no? What would you say?

She's the very image of propriety? A perfectly sane individual who sees nothing wrong in dragging her naïve niece into a gaming hell."

"I am not naïve."

He leaned back and glanced at the ceiling of the hack, shaking his head at the ribs and bent-board with peeling black paint. "Of course not. Begging your pardon. I nearly forgot. You're a sophisticated young lady. A woman well acquainted with all facets of life, able to extricate herself from the stickiest of situations." One side of his mouth curled up.

"I can see you grinning."

"I can remedy that." He pulled the black curtains, blocking out all but a trickle of outside light. "You shouldn't be observed in a hack anyway."

Willa humphed. "I don't see what difference it makes. I just attended Lady Vessmere's dubious charitable card party. I doubt there's anything left of my reputation to ruin."

"Which brings us back to your demented aunt. I cannot fathom what possessed her to take you into a gathering of that sort."

It was a sensible question. And yet it irked her sense of fair play. He ought not be there, if she should not. "You were there." She stared. Waiting for him to feel her jibe, hoping to see an ounce of shame.

"And what if I hadn't been?"

"That's not the point."

"Oh, but it is. What would have happened?"

She shrugged, as if it were of no consequence. "Then I suppose Lord Alberney might be dragging me upstairs."

"Precisely!" He jabbed his finger in the air, aiming it at her as if he planned to shoot a goose.

"Aha!" She leaned forward, shaking her finger at

him. "Then you admit there is an upstairs!" She'd trumped him. Although he didn't seem to realize it.

He stared at her as though she had just sprouted rabbit ears. "Of course, there is. You saw the staircase."

She warmed to their convoluted debate. "And have you been there? Up those stairs?"

"Willa, what are you talking about?" He didn't appear confused. A narrow line of lamplight snuck in around the edges of the curtain, beaming across his features. He looked pleased. Pleased she was jealous.

She had lost the debate. "You know perfectly well what I mean."

He arched one stultifying eyebrow.

How she wished she could do that.

He used the superior lilt of one who knows they've won the game. "I'm afraid you will have to clarify it for me. However, you might want to moderate your voice. The coachman can hear quite readily through these cloth walls without you shouting."

She would speak as loudly as she pleased. Who cares if the coachman heard? "Have you been in the widow's boudoir? That's what I mean. That awful Lady Vessmere. Is she one of your women?"

"Gad, Willa! Is that what you're on about?" He chortled happily and moved across the carriage to sit next to her. "No. I have never been in Lady Vessmere's lair." The devil stopped to rub his chin as if he must reconsider. "Although, I believe she was on the point of inviting me tonight. May have even done so. I'm not certain."

"Wretch!" Willa crossed her arms abruptly, but she had to know the rest. "Would you have gone?"

Both eyebrows flew up. "A lady is not supposed to ask those sorts of questions."

She set him her best stern expression. "Don't sidestep the matter."

His face softened and he lowered his voice. "No, Willa. I would not have gone." His gaze washed over her, cleansing away any doubt.

"Oh." It took only an instant for her relief to turn to consternation. She frowned. Why wouldn't he? The woman was undeniably attractive. Most men . . . but it made no sense. "Why not? Are your other women even more beautiful than she is?"

He made a soft whistling sound through his teeth and leaned his head in one hand, shaking it. "You need a proper chaperone. One who will school your tongue as well as keep you out of unsuitable places."

Pleased for some inexplicable reason, she took a deep breath. "I'm afraid it's too late for my tongue. There's no altering its education now. It follows my mind exactly, which was schooled to question everything. You may credit Socrates and our brothers for that."

He threw his hat across to the other seat and sat back, leaning his head against the back of the carriage. "Never would have believed I'd have to thank Daniel for anything. Yet, there it is."

"My tongue doesn't annoy you? A moment ago I thought you wanted someone to school it properly."

He stared at her. "A foolish thought. Why should I want to change something I enjoy so much?" Putting out his hand, he almost touched her, but didn't. "Your hair is coming loose."

"We are discussing my tongue not my hair, which you believe to be so woefully undisciplined it renders me socially unacceptable."

"Hhmm. Yes." He touched his finger to the curls beside her ear. "I'm not sure how will you get on in the world with such exceptional behaviors?"

He was not concentrating properly. She tried to recall his attention to the point. "Is that what you want? That I should get on in the world. Wear a white dress at proper parties and find an impoverished cleric willing to marry me despite my pitiful dowry?"

"At one time," he murmured, "I suppose I'd imagined such a thing. Have I told you that you look beautiful in blue?" He toyed with her hair, coiling and uncoiling his fingers in the curls falling down her neck. Then he drew his fingers along her bare shoulder to where he met with the dark blue cap of her puffed sleeves. "Lovely. I was certain I'd have to thrash Alberney to get him to let go of you."

She said nothing, but watched, captivated, as every stroke of his fingertips against her skin undressed his soul. She felt potent, powerful, and yet every layer of desire he revealed, vibrated against a twin within her. An invisible force linked them, like strings on an instrument tuned to the same note.

He pulled his hand away, squaring his shoulders, and adopted an authoritarian demeanor. "Lady Alameda should never have brought you there. She's unfit to chaperone *anyone,* let alone an innocent like you."

It took her a moment to absorb the meaning of his words, to drag her mind from the trance he'd invoked. She shook her head. "Aunt Honore would turn red and roar in your ear if she heard you call her *my chaperone.* I'm her protégée. She thinks of herself as my tutor."

"Exactly what is she tutoring you in, I wonder?" The coach had stopped briefly. He lifted the edge of the curtain and glanced out. "It doesn't matter what she calls herself, she's still your aunt. As such, she's woefully negligent in her duty toward you."

When the coach jolted back into motion Willa

bumped back against the seat. "Don't scold her overmuch. It could be worse."

"Worse? I cannot see how. The mad countess keeps thrusting you into risky situations without the least regard for your welfare. The very idea of taking you to Lady Vessmere's . . . well, I can only conclude the woman is a bedlamite."

Willa played with the silk of her skirt near her knees. It soothed her to rub the soft fabric between her thumb and middle finger. It harkened back to something in the shadowy memories of her infancy, perhaps the comforting folds of her mother's gown or a favorite blanket. She didn't know, but it reassured her. "The truth is, my aunt rescued me from what might have been endless years of dull . . . uneventful"—she tossed a hand into the air, resigned to honesty—"emptiness."

Emptiness? Alex stared, unseeing, into the dark cave of their hack. How could it be true of her who seemed so full? He sat beside her contemplating the vast difference between their lives. She was the good daughter. He the prodigal. That they should both have felt empty baffled him. "You disliked St. Cleve that much?"

"Disliked? No. St. Cleve is a pleasant-enough village. And I'm certain I will spend the rest of my days there in complete serenity."

"But? You said—"

She turned sharply, her lips pursed and when she pressed her fingers together, as if searching for patience with a slow student, he knew he was in for a lecture. "Serenity is a quality better appreciated after having experienced a few adventures and a bit of turmoil."

Turmoil? Such as the turmoil he felt in her presence. He doubted serenity was worth the price. He muttered, "I don't care to contemplate the sort of adventures you might have encountered tonight."

She said nothing.

Perhaps she underestimated the cost, nay the danger, of such an exploit. He turned to her. "You mustn't go into such places, Willa. You have no idea what might have befallen you. Promise me."

He was so earnest. She smiled. Willa wanted desperately to stroke her fingers through his hair. He looked like a little boy begging his puppy not to run out into the road.

"You mustn't worry. I amble about the world half blind, only rarely do I stumble or fall. I suspect it will be the same with this."

She couldn't resist. She slid her fingers into the curls over his ear.

He turned into her touch as if he enjoyed her petting him. A small motion for his part, but one which stirred heat within her body, weakening her and drawing her to him.

He whispered into her fingers. "You've never stumbled around London before." He caught her hand and kissed it as if they'd been friends forever. "It's that rare fall that disturbs me."

In the dim light, she stared at her hand caught in his. The sensation of his lips on her fingers still lingered in her mind. "Why does it disturb you?"

He grimaced. "Blast Socrates."

She no longer required the answer. It overjoyed her to witness his discomfort. "Would you really have thrashed Lord Alberney?"

"This is what comes of two old bachelors raising a girl. She asks too many questions."

She leaned toward him. "You might chastise my wicked tongue in other ways." She contemplated his mouth and concocted a very unladylike vision of herself tumbling into his arms and kissing him wildly. An idea fraught with logical flaws and potentially problematic consequences, but . . .

"Willa, what in heaven's name are you doing?" His voice was husky and close.

She caught herself, leaning into him, letting her wanton imaginings lead her. She fell back, embarrassed. "I'm sorry."

"Are you?" She peeked up at him; the wretch was grinning at her. "You're sorry? For what offense?"

She detested that knowing grin. It meant he could tell exactly what she had been contemplating. She humphed at him. "You truly are a wicked man."

"Quite so. Exceedingly wicked. A rascal of the first water. Did I not give you a list of my defects when we first met?"

She tapped her cheek. "Oh, yes. Now I remember. The consummate scoundrel, you said." She crossed her arms. "If that is so, why must you confuse me by showing me such kindness?"

"Folderol. I did no such thing. Not a kind bone in my body." He shook his finger at her. "Ah, but you are cleverly diverting me from the question, my dear. *Why* are you sorry?"

"You know perfectly well."

"Wouldn't ask, if I knew."

"Flummery. I can see it in your eyes. You know exactly what I was thinking."

He gently brushed his knuckles against her cheek and laughed softly.

She ought to pull away from him, but what would such discipline cost? The loss of his hand against her face. Too great a price. "It's laughable, isn't it? A silly little peahen like myself wanting to throw herself in your arms. It defies reason."

His fingers trailed down the side of her face, onto her neck, and he whispered, "You're not a peahen, Willa." He traced the outline of the sapphire necklace. A sliver of moonlight slanted across them as he trailed his fingers over her flesh, following the curve of the necklace almost to its conclusion.

She couldn't breathe until he brought his fingers back up beside her chin.

She swallowed hard, aware that she was acting the fool again. "Alex, it is as if you hold some magical power over me. Whenever I'm around you I feel compelled to kiss you. Are all rakes this skillful?"

"Is that what you think?" His features hardened and he took away his enchanted fingers, which had been so deftly tantalizing her neck. "I'm a rake? A seducer of women?"

"You needn't take umbrage. Haven't you instructed me to think the worst? And yes! I'm quite certain you have scores of women, women like Lady Vessmere, only more attractive and not so selfish in temperament. Dancers with almond eyes, tinkling cymbals, and veils—"

"A harem?" He fell back against the seat and laughed out loud.

"Shhh! The coachman will hear you. Pray, do not laugh at me. I know whereof I speak. I've read books on the subject and, naturally, when you said you were a rake and a scoundrel, I thought—"

"You must have read about a sheik."

She thumped her hand against the cracked leather of the seat. "Sheik, rake, it makes no difference. You both are vastly experienced with women."

He yanked on his cravat, pulling it free, and slid it up onto his head, sucking in his cheeks. "Do I look like a Bedouin?"

"Take that off."

He let it fall, draping around his neck, and crossed his arms. "Aside from that, if you will put that magnificent mind of yours to work, you will recall I have always denied being a rake."

"Yes, but—"

He glanced sideways at her. "Do you think me so depraved, that I would intentionally seduce you? An innocent?"

She bowed her head. What had she been thinking? Or had she merely been hoping? When all the while he had shown her nothing but kindness and consideration.

"No, of course not," she whispered. "Please. Forgive my rudeness. You're a gentleman, and have always treated me accordingly. It's just that when I'm near you I feel so . . ."

She grasped his folded arms. "Forgive me, Alex. It was merely the wild imaginings of a foolish girl."

He answered so softly, she barely heard him. "No, Willa. Not foolish. I felt it too."

Silence, not unpleasant, clip-clopped inside the coach. But in her mind there were shrieks of joy, horns sounding, drums beating, and whirling, twirling, dancing. *He felt it too.*

Alex took her hand in his, playing with her fingers one by one. "I wonder if *you* are not the one using mysterious enchantments on me." He kissed her palm, smoothed his hand over her naked forearm and sighed. "I've never felt this . . . *compelled* before either. Troublesome, is it not?"

He smiled teasingly. "Confess, Miss Linnet. Are you

a skilled seductress? Have our elder brothers been teaching you mystical arts of some kind?"

She tried to laugh but couldn't. She took a deep breath. "Naught but Socrates and Plato, Pythagorean theories and the golden mean."

"Ah, dead Greeks. I might have known." He curved his hand around her cheek.

She responded as he had, turning her lips to his palm and kissing it.

"How then, did you become so alluring?"

Taunts. Were these merely taunts he was laying at her feet? She shook her head. Caring little that by now her ridiculous hair must be springing riotously in nineteen different directions. She cared only for him. And for this moment, which would be lost forever if she didn't act.

She lowered her lashes. "If I had any skill at all, you would have been kissing me long ago, almost the moment we left Lady Vessmere's house."

He inhaled sharply and she knew she'd been far too brazen.

"Confound it, woman! How do you expect me to keep my distance if you say such things?"

Too mortified to speak, she sank back into the seat, hiding her face, unable to apologize. If she had to put words on her disgraceful attempt to seduce him and her abysmal failure, she would shed tears. Far too revealing tears.

He reached out to tuck a strand of wayward hair behind her ear. "No, don't think that. Come here, Willa." He pulled her into his arms.

She curled against his chest. "Alex, it's true. I'm afraid I'm the wicked one. I can't help it. Truly. I realize it isn't rational behav—"

"Shh." He touched his finger to her lips, and followed that by kissing her slowly, languidly.

When he pulled back, she felt bereft, grieved for want of his mouth on hers. She pulled him back to her lips so that he might taste her hunger.

He kissed her again. This time as if he felt the same craving she did. He held her so close, and kissed her so thoroughly, she could no longer tell the difference between her heart pounding, or his. His breath rising and falling, or hers.

He kissed the side of her neck, and along the sensitive slope on her shoulder.

A sound came unbidden out of her mouth, the mew of a kitten, or something equally foolish. Foolish because it made him stop.

Alex exhaled loudly. Leaning his head back, he ran his hand through his hair. "Dear God. Perhaps I am depraved."

"No!" She cupped his face in her palms. "You are the most wonderful man I've ever known. I want you to kiss me more and more." She felt excited, eager, like a child about to open a Christmas package.

He shook his head slightly, warily. "Willa, you don't know what you're asking of me."

She looked at him steadily. "I know precisely what I'm asking."

"In that case, my wicked little seductress, you ought to be spanked soundly. It isn't in my nature to be so well behaved. Resisting temptation is not my strong suit."

She caressed the rough shaven texture of his jaw. "Don't you understand? I would have withered into an old crone and never known this incredible happiness, had you not come into my life." She smiled. "Having tasted bliss, can you blame me for wanting more?" She leaned up and kissed him softly next to his ear. "There will never be another chance for me."

"That's not true, Willa. You're the sort who marries and raises a half-dozen children."

"Highly improbable."

He grabbed her hands and clasping them firmly in his, turned teacher. "Statistics and equations again? Let me assure you, it will happen. You will make some man excessively happy."

She shook her head, lowering it mournfully.

"And why not?" He lifted her chin, making her look at him, forcing her to memorize the silver light moving across his features, glistening against the dark of his eyes, falling across the slope of his nose, defining the strong lines of his jaw.

Because, I love you.

She couldn't tell him that. He might toss her out of the carriage. "Because . . ." She shook her head. "No, it's simply unthinkable." And it was.

"You're more beautiful than you realize. Surely—"

She sighed and sat up, facing him squarely. He may as well know the truth. If he tossed her out, so be it. "Whether I am beautiful or not is irrelevant. The thought of anyone but you touching me causes a sickness in my stomach. I don't believe I could abide it."

Alex swallowed hard. His gaze strayed to her breasts. The ridiculously low neckline did little to conceal her.

Willa felt completely naked. He was thinking of it then, someone else fondling her. Good, she could see it sickened him as well. His face blanched and hardened, like it had the night Darley almost died.

She fidgeted with the buttons on his vest. "You see my dilemma?"

He didn't answer. He was thinking. Contemplating what? The noise of it almost deafened her. His breathing was shallow and labored. She chewed the corner of her lip. What if he came to the wrong conclusion?

She had to take the advantage while she had it. Willa kissed him. She kissed his fine straight nose, his brow, his temple, his eyelids, closed tightly against her onslaught, and then she returned to his agreeable mouth.

She was wicked and, undoubtedly, foolish. But it no longer mattered.

He reached for her. With a touch, soft as the moonlight drifting into the window, he held her shoulder. Halting her. Clenching his jaw as if in pain. When he opened his eyes, Alex focused only on her face. "Do you trust me, Willa?"

Her voice broke. The small word came out in two hesitant pieces. "Yes."

"Are you certain?"

"You know that I do. That night Darley foaled I saw . . . I knew . . . It was as if I could see into your—"

He nodded and laid two fingers against her lips to keep her from saying more. "Then you must understand. It cannot be like this."

The carriage skidded, and jolted to a sudden stop, as if narrowly avoiding a collision. Someone yanked the door open.

Willa started when she recognized her brother's face framed in the lamplight of the open door. "Jerome! What are you doing here?"

"Protecting my sister. Unhand her, you cur!"

Alex swore.

"No," Willa insisted. "You don't understand. It's not what it seems." She quickly tried to stuff some of her recalcitrant hair back up into the ribbons.

"I can see well enough what's what." Jerome's voice echoed with condemnation.

Just then Sir Daniel stuck his head into the doorway and squinted into the dark coach. "Alex, how could you do this?"

"For pity sake! He didn't do anything. He saved me from an excessively difficult situation. If you will both calm down and let me explain."

"Enough, Willa," Jerome commanded. "We listened to your defense of this scoundrel the other day and it won't wash." Jerome slapped his hand against the door frame. "The facts speak quite eloquently on the matter of his character. Now get out of that coach this instant."

As if the whole world must witness this insanity, Aunt Honore wriggled in between the two men. Willa wondered if this was one of those maniacal dreams, the kind suddenly overcrowded with exactly the wrong people at the worst possible moment.

Her aunt smiled serenely. "Good evening, m'dear. I take it you were not enthralled with the Widow Vessmere's card party? Come. My carriage awaits."

"Not a bit of it." Jerome put out his hand, barring the way, not that Willa had moved as yet. "She's coming with me."

"Oh?" Honore arched her eyebrow. (A distinctly useful feature, perhaps if Willa practiced in the mirror she might learn how.) "You want Willa to come with you? And where are you lodging, Jerome? Bachelor's quarters, no doubt. No female servants. Not at all suitable for a young lady, is it?"

Willa edged toward the open door as Jerome sputtered ineffectually at their aunt.

Alex spoke in a low voice as she stepped past him. "I'll repair this. Trust me, Willa."

She had no idea what he meant, but she knew the whole ordeal was her fault. "I should never have—"

Honore grasped Willa's hand and firmly tugged her

out of the hack. "Do lower your voice, Jerome. Take a look about you. We're not the only ones on the street. Would you have Willa's reputation in tatters by morning?"

Jerome stood his full height and enunciated in clear ringing tones, "I fear you have already done a job of that. I've merely come to salvage what is left of my sister's life."

Honore managed to guide Willa behind her. "Nonsense. As your friend Wordsworth says, you're making much ado about nothing."

Jerome pinched up his face in disgust. "Not Wordsworth."

Daniel nodded. "No, indeed. Shakespeare."

"Either way. Still making a lion's den out of a molehill. There's the carriage, Willa." She gave her a little shove. "Go along."

Willa heard Alex rap on the ceiling of the coach as she hurried toward her aunt's vehicle. She glanced back over her shoulder. His hack slipped artfully around the cabriolet that had waylaid them and took off at a rapid clip with the open door still flapping wildly.

Sir Daniel ran out into the street, waving his arms, trying to summon his fleeing brother back to the scene. Jerome stood, mouth agape, on the curb like a cleric without a prayer. As she walked away, Honore invited him to visit Alison Hall on the morrow for a less public tête-à-tête.

Willa hurriedly climbed into the calm, dark sanctuary of her aunt's carriage. If she had truly believed she must have turmoil to appreciate the serenity of St. Cleve, she had her wish now.

19

And She Called for Her Fiddlers Three

Lady Alameda's white-haired butler showed Alex into a sunny breakfast room. A huge mural of the Roman countryside graced one wall. The windows on the other side were draped in butter yellow silk. The lady herself sat at the end of a long table, pouring over the society columns of the *Post,* while munching on a slice of toasted bread and jam. She scarcely looked up when the butler announced him.

"Come." She signaled. "Sit. Eat."

The sideboard was arranged with enough food for a dozen men: kippers and sausages, eggs and curds, muffins and fruit. Alex declined. He was not here to fill his belly.

"I've come to ask for Willa's hand in marriage."

She glanced up. "And why would you do that? A man like you doesn't want a wife shackled to his leg. Put a crimp in your activities, I should think." She set her toast on her plate and wiped her hands on the pristine white tablecloth, inspecting him with undisguised interest.

Alex stood at attention. "Surely, after last night, it's no less than my duty as a gentleman."

"Oh that." She waved her hand. "Duty. Can't abide it."

He had no doubt of that. "There are some of us who take it rather more seriously than others."

Her brow lifted as if he'd angered her, but she smirked. "You? Are *you* ringing a small peal over my head, young Braeburn?"

He declined to answer.

"Yes"—she drew it out—"I do believe you are." She laughed. "Quite right, too. Ought not to have taken the gel to Lady Vessmere's house, eh? Is that the set of your jib? Put you in a bundle of trouble, did I?" She stabbed a sausage and contemplated it on the end of her fork. "Well, you needn't worry. I've dealt with the matter. You are absolved, my son. Go and sin no more." She waved the sausage in a partial sign of the cross.

"Taken up the priesthood have you?"

She snorted. "Perhaps, I ought."

"Nevertheless, I should like to pay my addresses to Willa. The matter may be of more import to her, than yourself."

"I wonder." She bit the sausage and peered at him shrewdly.

Alex disliked the way she watched his face for the slightest hint of weakness. He'd seen that look in pickpockets and thieves. He kept his expression intentionally unyielding.

She tapped her fingernails on the edge of the table, slowly, markedly, tallying each strike against him. "Tell me, exactly what would you *do* with a wife? Closet her on a farm in Suffolk somewhere, and run off to play with your friends in Town? I cannot think such an arrangement would be amenable to Willa."

"I wouldn't . . ." But what would he do? He hadn't gotten that far in his thinking. He knew only that Willa's reputation was ruined, and he was to blame. That, and the fact that the thought of anyone else having her made his blood churn.

"You wouldn't what?" She cocked her head sideways, a vulture deciding if its quarry was dead enough to peck apart. She shrugged. "Still, duty is such a distasteful premise for a marriage, wouldn't you say?" She dropped the remainder of the sausage onto her plate and stood up.

"I have every intention of treating her properly."

"Ah, proper intentions." She swished toward him. "A noble sentiment. I hadn't thought you—"

An uproar in the hallway distracted her. "What in blazes?"

Harry charged in, with the butler close on his heels, trying to prevent him from entering the room.

Harry went straight to Alex. "What are you doing here, you scoundrel? Lecher! How could you! And after all your fine speeches about her being an innocent. The vicar's little sister, you said. A closed carriage! Ruined her reputation. Whole town's talking of it."

Alex wondered if he'd fallen asleep and awakened trapped in one of Shakespeare's more confusing plays. "What are you doing here, Harry?"

Harry took a breath and tugged his waistcoat down. The gray silk vest had a way of folding up at the point of Harry's fullest girth. He cleared his throat and stuck his finger into the air, exactly like a preacher pointing to the omnipotence of the Almighty. In a booming voice he announced, "I will defend her honor."

He strode up to Alex and slapped him across the cheek with a long riding glove.

Alex pressed his lips together and glanced up at the ceiling, trying to maintain his composure.

Harry bowed to Lady Alameda. "Your servant, my lady. Sorry to intrude. Couldn't be helped."

She opened her palms wide, gracefully bidding him entry. "Delighted to have your company, Mr. Erwin." She waved the piqued butler away. "May I offer you some breakfast?"

Harry glanced with interest at the generously laden sideboard. "Perhaps later I might indulge." But he pulled himself up short and stopping leaning in the direction of the food. "Pressing matters, you know." He turned back to Alex. "What say you? I'm calling you out. Pistols at dawn."

Alex sincerely wished his friend had succumbed to the kippers. "Don't be ridiculous. I'm not going to fight you, Harry. Although if you care to stand for a few bouts at Jackson's I won't deny you."

He rubbed his chin. "No. Won't serve the purpose. Must be shown a lesson. Boxing me won't do it. Pistols at dawn. Nothing else will do."

Lady Alameda moved back to her place at the table and lifted her teacup and saucer. "I believe the choice of weapons belongs to your opponent. Is that not proper form, Mr. Braeburn?" She took a sip of her morning tea.

Harry sputtered. "Oh? Oh, yes. Right you are. Well, then. What will it be, Alex? Despoiling maidens—calls for blood of some kind."

"Don't be an ass. I didn't despoil her."

"Not an ass. Defending her honor. A first-rate gel. Happy to marry her too, after I dispose of you." He turned to Lady Alameda and bowed again. "With your permission of course, my lady."

She set her teacup down. "So many offers in one

morning. Rather like an auction isn't it? I'm quite overcome." She didn't look overcome. She appeared to be highly entertained, like a child at the fair, watching the dancing bears. "Which one shall I choose? Dear me. Such a quandary."

Realization occurred slowly as Harry added up the sum of her words. He frowned at Alex. "You asked already?"

Alex inclined his head. Flexing his jaw, biting back any number of colorful oaths threatening to escape his lips.

"Beat me to it? Hardly sporting. She can't want you. You're the wretch that ruined her. Aside from that, you've no ambition beyond your horses." Harry crossed his arms and shut his eyes as if the matter were settled ad infinitum. "I daresay, she won't have you."

Alex inhaled loudly. "No. I pale tragically in the shadow of your numerous qualifications. Nevertheless, the duty falls to me. As you say, I'm the wretch who ruined her."

Lady Alameda tapped her finger against her lips. "There's that niggling word again. So unlovely is *duty*." She grimaced at Alex, crinkling her nose up, as if the mere word reeked like a dead cat moldering in a closet.

She turned at the sound of raised voices and clattering in the hallway. "Oh dear, now who could that be?" But Alex suspected she already knew.

Jerome charged into the breakfast room, waving a piece of paper. The elderly butler tried to restrain him by tugging on his sleeve, and Daniel followed meekly in their wake.

"Let them in, Cairn. Let them in." Lady Alameda waved them forward.

The harried butler threw his hand in the air and turned on his heel.

"Jerome, my dear, how lovely to see you. What is it? Another *alarming letter*?" Her voice took on false gravity. Alex observed the recalcitrant play at the corner of her mouth.

Jerome, oblivious of her jibe, was in high dudgeon. "No. This is a special marriage license. Where's Willa? Where is she? Up half the night getting this thing. Best solution all round."

Lady Alameda clucked her tongue. "Oh, but, my dear, when last I checked, it was against the law and quite frowned upon to marry your sister. Do have some breakfast and reconsider."

"What? Good heavens, no! Not me. Him." He pointed at his hapless companion.

Daniel glared at Alex. "It's the least I can do after the shame my brother has brought upon her."

"Oh my. How very *noble* you are." Lady Alameda's hand fluttered to her breast in a little fanning motion, but she cast a sly look at Alex. "Extraordinarily noble."

Daniel bowed his head in assent. "Merely my duty."

"Your du—oo—ty?" Lady Alameda dragged out the word, relishing every newly invented syllable. She smiled pertly. "How very like your brother you are. But, I'm afraid, these two gentlemen have preceded you."

"You?" Daniel glanced at Alex in astonishment and lapsed almost immediately into his customary skepticism. "And you actually intend to go through with it?"

Alex stared at his brother steadily and refused to honor his insult with a reply. Let Daniel stew in his own scorn.

"Hey ho. See here, I'm the one who loves her." Harry thumped his chest with his palm and thumb as if he were clearing out a cough. "Me! No need for all this fuss. I'll put a bullet in Alex at dawn tomorrow. That satisfies the question of her reputation. Then Miss Linnet and I will tie the knot. Nothing could be simpler."

Jerome studied Harry with interest. "And who might you be?"

Alex decided to perform the introductions. "A jackanapes, to whom you should pay no attention."

"Here now. No way to speak of your friends?" Harry looked truly injured. "I'm a perfectly respectable gentleman. Mr. Harry Erwin, at your service." He grasped Jerome's hand and pumped it enthusiastically. "Not a pauper, sir. Good family. Your sister might be comfortably situated as my wife."

Daniel's eyes narrowed in a mercenary glint. Jerome leaned interestedly toward Harry.

Alex didn't care for the direction their wheels were turning. He decided it was time to put an end to their speculation. "Unfortunately, Harry, you might be dead come sunrise, unless you withdraw this absurd challenge."

Lady Alameda smiled wryly. "Oh yes, quite true. Where do you plan to carry out this little duel? I should be most interested in the outcome."

Harry shuffled uneasily. "Don't know. I expect the seconds decide all those details."

"Allow me to spare you the suspense." Alex paused to make sure they were all attending carefully. "Swords. In Squire Russell's east field."

"Swords! You know I can't fence more than a farthing's worth." Harry tugged at his ill-fitting vest once more.

Alex shrugged. "The choice is mine. However, if you will withdraw, nothing need be said."

"Dueling is forbidden." Daniel glared at Alex. "Now you intend to add murder to your list of crimes."

Alex managed to keep the anger out of his voice. "What is one more crime among so many?"

Daniel shook his head. "Reprehensible."

"As always." Alex inclined his head.

"Saber or foil?" Harry scuffed the toe of his shoe against the marble tile. "Don't really fancy saber. Blade leaves a nasty wound."

"As opposed to a bullet?" Alex crossed his arms and walled himself off from the entire host of lunatics populating Lady Alameda's breakfast room.

Apparently, Jerome had more important things on his mind than swords or pistols. He tapped his chin and spoke specifically to Lady Alameda. "This is all very confusing. Am I to understand both of these gentlemen have offered for Willa?"

Lady Alameda raised her hands palms outward. "So it would seem."

He laid the special license on the table and laced his fingers behind his back. Clearly, the man wanted to pace as he pondered the events of the morning, but Lady Alameda blocked his path.

"Do have some breakfast, Jerome."

He shook two fingers at his aunt, declining her offer. "Tell me, what has Willa to say to any of this?"

"I haven't the slightest notion." Lady Alameda appeared completely unconcerned. She plucked a muffin from the buffet and spread butter liberally atop it.

"We must send for her. So we can see which one she wants."

"Oh, I hardly think that would be prudent, do you? After all, she's far too young to know her mind on matters as grave as these." She chomped unabashedly into the muffin.

Grave? Alex didn't like it. There was mockery in her tone. She was up to something.

Jerome muttered and attempted once again to pace. "Hhmm. Usually she's far too opinionated on most matters, if anyone was to ask me."

One small corner of Alex's mouth curled up. Thank God for that, Willa *was* opinionated. She wouldn't agree easily to any arrangement other than one she approved.

Lady Alameda finished another bite of muffin and brushed the crumbs from the front of her gown. "Aside from that, the matter does not lie entirely in her hands. Suppose that our dear Willa has her heart set on Mr. Erwin, here." She laid her hand on the poor devil's shoulder. "It's quite possible that Mr. Braeburn will run him through before breakfast tomorrow. Surely, you see the complexity of the situation?"

Harry blanched. "Don't like the sound of that. Change to pistols, Alex. Sporting thing for a chum to do."

"Chums don't usually challenge one another to a duel."

Harry sighed. "Wouldn't want to kill your best friend, would you? Might tear Miss Linnet's heart to shreds."

"Good grief, Harry. I have no desire to do either one. Would you rather I allow *you* to shoot *me*? In which case, you might very well spend an interesting twenty years in Australia."

"Would've aimed high."

Alex fought a growing impulse to shake his friend till the dunderhead's teeth rattled. "I've gone shooting with you, Harry. If you aim high, very likely, you'll strike me square between the eyes."

Harry began to bluster about the accuracy of his aim, while Alex did his best to ignore him.

Jerome picked up the special license again and fidgeted with it while looking askance at Daniel. "There's only one way to settle this. I would like to speak with my sister. Lady Alameda, if you would be so kind?"

"Happy to oblige you, except she isn't here." She popped the remainder of the muffin into her mouth and chewed happily.

All four men looked at her as if something peculiar had just crept into the room.

"Not here?" Alex narrowed his gaze on the conniving countess. What was she up to?

She shook her head and smiled serenely, all the while looking like a young child caught stealing sweets.

Jerome paced impatiently. "Very well. When do you expect her?"

Lady Alameda licked the butter from her lips before answering. "A day. Two. Or perhaps three. Certainly, no more than a fortnight, I should think. She's visiting friends."

"Might've told me," Jerome protested weakly.

Lady Alameda shrugged. "She left rather suddenly."

Harry sniffed, a wounded sort of sniff. "Won't even know about the duel, will she? Perhaps, we ought to wait till she comes back."

She straightened to her full height, shook out her skirts, and beamed at Harry, just as if they were discussing an upcoming dinner party. "Oh no, if you think her honor needs defending what purpose would it serve to wait? Sunrise tomorrow suits me perfectly. I have nothing else on my schedule at that hour."

Harry looked at her, alarmed. "Can't mean to watch, can you? Not the thing for a lady. What with the blood and horror of it all." He shuddered.

"Fiddle-faddle, I wouldn't dream of missing it. I'm not the squeamish sort. A little blood never hurt anyone."

"No," Harry muttered softly. "It's the lack of it that worries me."

"Good. I'm glad that's settled." Lady Alameda clapped her hands together. "You gentlemen may as well help yourself to some sustenance while you are here. Now, if you will excuse me, I have several pressing business matters to attend to."

"But we haven't settled anything." Jerome held out the special license, which drooped as she walked past him. She strode briskly out, leaving them all standing uncomfortably in her breakfast room.

Daniel picked up a plate and selected a half-dozen sausages, a kipper, and two eggs. When he turned to discover that they were all staring at him, he explained without the slightest chagrin, "A pity to allow it to go to waste."

"Come along, Harry." Alex patted his stout friend on the shoulder. "Who have you named as your second?"

"Don't know. Tournsby is still convalescing. Can't very well ask him."

"What say we retire to the club and see who we might conscript into service?"

With any luck, Alex surmised, before the night was out he would have Harry so foxed the fellow wouldn't remember his own name let alone this ridiculous duel.

20

The Sticking Point

Adieu the clang of war's alarms!
To other deeds my soul is strung,
And sweeter notes shall now be sung;
My harp shall all its powers reveal,
To tell the tale my heart must feel;
Love, Love alone, my lyre shall claim,
In songs of bliss and sighs of flame.

Excerpt from *Anacreon*
by Lord Byron

Alex squinted with considerable irritation at the sun just beginning to breach the horizon. "I cannot fathom why you got out of bed."

"Matter of honor. Had to." Harry was wearing the same soiled garments he had slogged around in the night before. His chin could use a good scraping, and as to his brain, Alex doubted there was anything that could be done.

"There's no one here, Harry. It isn't legal without our seconds. Come to think of it, it isn't legal in either case."

Harry crossed his arms defensively. "Well, I don't see *your* man on the field? Thought Davies was good for it?"

Alex pinched the bridge of his nose. "He was. Given the advanced state of your inebriation last night, I told him not to trouble himself. This is an inhuman hour to ask a friend to rise unnecessarily."

"As it turns out, it was necessary." Harry cocked his chin up, looking rather too pleased with himself.

Alex, on the other hand, was not pleased. Harry ought to be blissfully snoring in the tousled comfort of his featherbed, completely unaware of the hour. "And your man, Harry? Where do you suppose he got off to?"

Harry scratched at his morning's growth of whiskers. "Can't for the life of me remember who I asked."

"Hhmm. Evidently, neither can he." Alex flexed his foil and tested it in the air next to Harry's shoulder. "Where's the surgeon? Who did you expect would sew you up afterward?"

"Dunno." Oblivious of the *phft phft* of Alex's sword whipping near his ear, Harry bent over and adjusted one of his sagging stockings. "Didn't get that far in m'thinking. Doesn't one's second attend to that?"

"Apparently." Alex frowned at the empty field. "See here, Harry, I have no desire to injure you. Why don't you deal me a scratch on the arm? You'll have drawn first blood. Willa's honor will be defended. And we can both go home to bed."

Harry brightened considerably. He cradled his foil as he mulled it over. But then his features sagged unhappily. "Not sure it's quite the thing, Alex. Will the lady believe I did my utmost to settle the score, if you merely have a nick on the arm?"

Alex was beginning to lose patience. "Based upon my knowledge of the young lady's character, if Willa knew we were planning a duel she would be standing in this very field shaking her finger in our faces."

Harry chuckled. "You may be right there. A fiery maid, if ever there was one. Have you ever seen a gel so forthright and honest?" He waxed all balmy and soft-eyed, resting his sword point on the ground in the vain attempt to lean on his sword.

"No. Never met a woman like her." Alex exhaled loudly. "And now that we've established that—Harry, kindly do not abuse the sword. It's not a shovel, or a cane. You'll dull the point. I imagine you want to keep it sharp. How else do you expect to run me through?"

Harry tipped up the blade, flicked the dirt off it, and wiped the point on his shirtsleeve. "It'll do."

Alex had a sudden desire to skewer something, rather than stand idle in this field all morning with mosquitoes biting his ankles. He eyed Harry, and inhaled slowly, deliberately. "I seriously doubt she'll be pleased with either one of us if we do any significant damage to each other."

"See your point." Harry's red nose bobbed up and down as he agreed. "Don't want to put her off me by wounding you too badly."

Harry? Wound him? He glowered at the sun rising over the hills, burning through the low clouds. Alex's skill with the sword was well known in the clubs of London. Why was Harry gammoning himself?

Ah, the delusions a woman can cause in the mind of a man.

Alex need only look at the foolishness brewing in his own head. Could he truly cope with the responsibilities of being a husband? A month ago, he would not have laid odds on it. And yet now the thought failed to send him galloping off in the other direction. Instead, a pleasant sense of contentment settled on him.

He smiled and shrugged out of his coat. Time to get down to business. "Your choice, Harry, old boy. I'm offering you my arm." He rolled up his sleeve. "If you refuse, I'll be happy to oblige you in any manner you choose. Perhaps you would prefer some scoring on your cheek? A dramatic zigzag? You might wear it as a badge of honor the rest of your days. Or, as the bloodthirsty countess suggested, I can send you up to discuss it with St. Peter. Your move."

Alex shoved his sleeve up as high as it would go and leaned his arm sideways, within easy reach of Harry's foil.

Harry glanced away. In the distance, a carriage rattled wildly up the road, kicking up a dust even in the morning mist.

There was no direct sun. Nevertheless, Harry shaded his bleary eyes. "Halloo, what's this? I don't believe it. The countess is coming to see for herself?"

Alex sighed. "Precisely what it needs. A meddling matriarch."

Alex and Harry stood about a furlong away from the road, watching the coach approach. It hadn't even come to a complete stop when the door flew open and an occupant frantically spilled out, tumbling to her hands and knees from off the last step. The woman inelegantly scrambled to her feet and started to scream.

Alex shook his head, confused. It was not the demented Countess Alameda. Unless he missed his guess, the old woman running erratically toward them, mobcap askew, was Willa's housekeeper from the vicarage.

"What in heaven's name is that?" Harry asked.

But Alex had already dashed off to meet the frantic maid.

She stumbled, weaving crazily as she ran, waving both arms at him. "Stop. Mr. Braeburn, stop! Don't kill him, sir! You've got to help me first. She's in trouble."

By the time Alex reached her, she was doubled over, out of breath and shaking. Yet she rattled on like a hundred-year-old coach and six. "I warned Willa. But would she listen to her old Aggie? No. Headstrong little mite. Won't pay proper heed." She coughed, her thin body quaking violently with the effort.

Alex offered her the support of his arm. "How may I be of service, Aggie? What's happened to Willa?"

"Oh, sir." She grabbed his arm with both hands and gripped him with the ferocity of a frightened hawk. "I told Willa we shouldn't trust the likes o' that Lady Alameda. An aunt like that, phah!" She made a pretense at spitting. "Should be hung at Tyburn, if anyone was to ask me. As it is, I'm probably the one what'll hang. Bribed her coachman to bring me here, I did. Abstracting her ladyship's coach is bound to be a hanging crime, e'en it?"

He frowned, trying to sort through her gibberish. "Absconding?"

She put a hand protectively up to her neck. "I had to do it. Had to get help for my Willa. She won't know how to fight off the likes of a womanizing lord like him. That's why I had to take her ladyship's carriage."

"Yes, yes. Of course you did. No one will fault you for that. Now, please! Tell me the rest."

Harry bounded up beside them, huffing and puffing. "What's to do?"

Aggie glanced at him cursorily and turned back to Alex. "Wasn't enough time to send for the vicar. I overheard them say you were coming here, to Battersea, to kill someone. And afterward, you'd have to ship off to Australia, or be hanged, and the plump fellow would be dead, and then that awful—"

"Hear now!" Harry objected to her forecast of the duel. "I might've prevailed."

"Harry!" Alex shot him a warning glance. "Let her speak, man. Willa is in trouble."

"Oh! Yes. Right ho." He patted the frail woman on her shoulder. "And then?" Harry urged Aggie onward. "Then that awful . . . what?"

Aggie nodded vigorously. "Yes, awful! Oh, I wish we'd stayed in St. Cleve. Nothing bad ever 'appens there."

She was about to break into a bawl. Alex had to find out what was happening to Willa. He dropped his sword to the ground and grasped Aggie by the shoulders. "Where is Willa? What happened?"

"They were talking in the hall. Her, the countess an' that bleedin' Scottish witch. Sayin' as how he was a fortune hunter—with naught but lint in his pockets, sir. And my Willa, she's there—where he is. And seeing as how he's wanting her money he'll try to compromise our Willa, he will. That's what they said, laughin', like it was all a grand lark. But when he discovers she has naught but a pittance, he'll cast her off. I comes out into the hall, I did. They turned up as mum as two dead cats, they did. Wicked, unnatural—"

Alex gave up hoping for a rational explanation and shook her. "Who? Who's going to compromise Willa?"

Aggie looked at him, startled by his sharp tone. "Why it's that horrid Lord Tournsby."

"Tournsby?" He mouthed the name.

She nodded, mute for the first moment in fifteen.

He should have guessed. Willa had gone to stay at Lady Tricot's with Alfreda. Tournsby, the wretch, would have ample of opportunity to devise a situation that would compromise her.

"Mr. Braeburn?" Aggie jostled his arm. "Sir, I beg you. I don't know who else to ask. Please, won't you save our little Wilhemina? She hasn't never done a wrong thing in her whole life." Her mouth twisted in a grimace. "Mayhaps, that isn't exactly true. But she's a good girl! A good girl, Mr. Braeburn. And she needs protecting."

"Yes! Yes." Alex raked his hand through his hair, trying to think.

Harry slapped him on the back. "I say, Alex, we've got to do something. Can't just stand about—"

"Right. Hold steady." Alex tipped up Harry's foil so that the point was aimed directly at his arm. He grasped the end of it and pressed it into his bicep. Harry paid no attention to Alex, but nattered on about which road would carry them most speedily to Lady Tricot's estate.

Alex pulled the point across the skin of his upper arm, drawing a line of blood across his bunched muscles.

"What's this? You're bleeding, Alex!" Harry fumbled with his sword while digging for his handkerchief.

"Yes. Now, you've met your obligation. The lady's honor is satisfied." Alex grabbed up his weapon from the grass and marched toward his horse, leaving Harry standing behind him, mouth hanging open like a coal bin.

"Wait a bit!" Harry shouted, "I'm coming too."

"And me!" Aggie added.

If they intended to come, they'd jolly well better start running because he wasn't about to wait for either of them. He climbed on his horse.

Harry ran after him, handkerchief waving in the wind. "Can't go without me. Don't forget, I'm to be the bridegroom."

Alex shoved his sword into a sheath on his saddle. "Don't be a fool, Harry. You can't marry her. She loves me."

Harry thundered up to Alex's horse. "Don't matter. Gels change their feelings like the tide. She'll come round"—he wheezed, trying to catch up his wind—"once she sees you're not the marrying sort."

Alex wheeled his horse toward the road. "That's where you're wrong, Harry."

"Well, I'll take my chances. Deuced tired, but I'm coming with you. See if I don't." Harry bent over, breathing heavily, hands on his knees. "What about Tournsby?"

Alex dug his heels in and directed his horse down the road toward the bridge. "I may have to run him through." A shame. But then, this seemed to be a day destined for killing his best friends.

21

Ring Around the Roses

Oh! Cease to affirm that man, since his birth,
From Adam till now, has with wretchedness
strove;
Some portion of paradise still is on earth
And Eden revives in the first kiss of love.

Excerpt from "The First Kiss of
Love," by Lord Byron, *Poems On
Various Occasions*, published 1807

He'd left his blasted coat hanging over a tree branch back in Battersea fields. Lady Tricot's white-wigged butler stared with distaste at the sizeable pool of drying blood on Alex's linen shirtsleeve.

"You heard me, man. Where is Miss Linnet? I'm not in a mood to be toyed with."

Indeed, if the blood didn't frighten the prim old goat, the sword Alex held tautly in his other hand ought to indicate his mood. Furious. Impatient. Gad, any fool could see it. He probably looked like an avenging angel who had flown out of the pit with Beelzebub. "Speak up! She's in danger."

"*Not* at the moment," the old man answered archly.

"Not danger from me, you idiot. I'm a friend." Alex pushed open the door and stomped into the foyer, using his height to cower the stubborn gatekeeper. "Now where is she?"

The butler held up his hands as if he might bar Alex's entry with a mere gesture. "I assure you, sir. I saw her myself, not more than a half hour ago. She was in perfectly good health. Now, if you will kindly—"

Alex thrust his sword point under the fellow's chin. "Do you see these muddy boots I'm wearing?"

The man squeaked affirmation without nodding his head.

"Yes, well, I've been slogging about a filth-infested field since before dawn. Riding like the hounds were after me for the rest of the morning. I'm tired. I'm hungry. And if I must tramp these soiled boots through every room in this house until I find Miss Linnet, I will. I'm that worried about her. Now, you may give me her direction. Or produce the young woman. Or summon Lady Tricot. She's bound to be more reasonable than her obstinate servant. Now, which will it be?"

Poor fellow. Without moving his head one whit, he glanced down at Alex's disgustingly grimy boots, and paled. "The garden," he whispered, squeezing his eyes shut. "The young lady is in the garden. Please, sir, around back."

"No tricks?" Alex inhaled deeply and pulled back his foil.

"No, sir." The butler shook his head, color returning to his cheeks. "But, if you would, kindly, take the path around the *outside* of the house?"

The fragrant roses meant nothing to him, as Alex marched directly around back to the gardens. Butterflies and birds were mere nuisances. He was a man ready for battle. A knight-errant on a quest.

He glimpsed his quarry in the gazebo. Although, he didn't have a clear view of the natty rogue. The opening faced away from him, providing its occupants with a tranquil view of the Thames as it flowed peacefully toward the sea.

He felt anything but tranquil.

A warrior does not like to spy his enemy down on one knee, orating flamboyantly to an unseen audience, in a lacy gazebo covered in thick, flowering vines, vines that must surely smell like honey. It is especially unsettling when the soldier glimpses skirts. Particularly vexing, if he's fairly certain those delicate flounces belong to the woman he loves.

Naturally, he charged forth. Sword in hand. Intent on rendering the conniving lord speechless for the rest of his misbegotten existence.

Alex grabbed Lord Tournsby by the throat and yanked him to his feet. "If you've so much as laid one finger on her I'll spit you like a Sunday goose."

Breathing like a bull on a rampage, Alex glowered into his captive's surprised face. A book toppled out of Tournsby's hand and thumped dully on the stone floor of the gazebo.

In a smooth, unperturbed, feminine voice, someone made a request. "If you will be so good as to let him finish the poem before you turn him into a goose, I would be much obliged."

The voice was familiar. It was not Willa's. Then he remembered. Alfreda. He loosened his grip slightly.

"Good heavens, Alex? I had no idea you disliked poetry so violently." Now, that was Willa.

He let go of Neddie's collar and spun around. The two women sat side by side on a bench, staring at him like he had sprouted horns. And maybe he had.

Willa squinted and jumped up. "Blood! You've been hurt."

Alex stared at her. "He's wooing you with poetry?" She grabbed his arm and began rolling up his sleeve to survey the damage.

"Not me, silly. Alfreda." She shook her head, struggling to push his sleeve further up his arm. "And very sloppy poetry, at that. It's Byron. What happened here?" She gently pressed the flesh underneath the wound, checking the depth of the cut.

He winced, but held steady. "Do you mean Neddie is courting Alfreda?" The tender movement of her fingers on his arm held him spellbound.

Tournsby, standing behind Alex, cleared his throat. "An angel, is she not? Just look at her. Hair like white silk. The carriage of a queen." He sighed. "Lay odds you never thought you'd see me reading poems."

Alfreda stood up and fluffed out her skirt. "Yes, and I quite like it." She picked up the fallen book, handing it back to Tournsby. "I find Byron's use of uneven rhythm in his verse unique and refreshing."

Willa sniffed skeptically. "A lazy writer. Undisciplined." She continued to examine the muscles around Alex's cut, brushing away flecks of dried blood. "I cannot blame you for wanting to put a stop to it. I fear I would've throttled him myself in another five minutes."

Tournsby put hand to heart and held out the book. In grossly overdone thespian inflections he read,

I hate you, ye cold compositions of art!
Though prudes may condemn me, and bigots reprove,
I court the effusions that spring from the heart,
Which throbs with delight to the first kiss of love.

Alfreda mewed her approval.

Tournsby continued to read.

Willa shook her head and added quietly, "You see what I have been suffering?"

Alex could not help but remember their first kiss. Perhaps Byron's poetry was not so poorly written after all. "I didn't come to rescue you from bad poems." He leaned down beside her ear, her corkscrew tendrils tickling his cheek, and whispered, "Aggie was certain you were in danger from Neddie."

"Lord Tournsby?" She chuckled. "Well, as you can see . . . but thank you all the same. Although, let me assure you, I am quite capable of managing the likes of him without assistance. I'm afraid it is *you* who pose the greater threat to my well-being." She looked at him squarely, without condemnation or malice, stating pure fact. "For I am bound to act a complete fool in your presence. Am I not?" It pierced him far deeper than a sword could ever do.

"Willa, I—"

She held up her hand, stopping the tide of his declarations with one small palm. "We must clean and dress this wound properly. It has reddened and I fear it may become infected."

"Yes, but—"

"How did you come by such a gash?" She poised her hands on her hips.

"It's nothing. Harry got some mutton-headed notion he needed to defend your honor."

"My honor? You mean, a duel? With Harry?" Sunlight caught on her red curls, flashing amber and hot coals. "Alex! You might have hurt him."

"What? Hurt *Harry*?" Alex indignantly yanked his sleeve back down, muttering oaths. "I was demmed lucky to escape with my sanity." He inhaled loudly. "Oh, look. Here comes your champion now."

"What's this?" Tournsby tore himself away from Byron and clapped Alex on the shoulder. "Didn't know you were inviting a party."

Alex merely growled.

Harry rounded the rosebushes and tromped down the path toward them, a bulldog with a prized bone in his teeth, carrying on loudly before he was even close enough to hear clearly. "Told you I'd get here, didn't I? Sent the hysterical maid home with Lady A's coach. Kept bawling about getting hung. Then had a devil of a time getting past that old prig of a butler. Had to threaten to puncture his liver if he didn't tell me straightway where you were. An accommodating fellow once I gave him the what's what."

Harry stopped to take a breath. He took stock of the company, doffed his hat to the ladies, and smiled amiably at them all, as if he'd just dropped in for afternoon tea.

He bowed low to Willa and cleared his throat. "Came to ask your hand, Miss Linnet. Pledge my undying affection." He slapped a thick paw across his chest. "Do me the honor."

Willa smiled at Harry so sympathetically, Alex half expected her to scratch the big old pup behind the ears.

Tournsby snorted. "Egad, Harry. Who let you out

of the attic? Stop acting like a cake. What happened, did you sleep in your clothes? You look a complete disaster."

Harry brandished his sword. "Tournsby, you blackguard! If Alex hasn't cut you to ribbons, I will."

Alex laid a hand on the blade, restricting the wobbling point from putting out anyone's eye. "At ease, Harry. The situation isn't quite as dire as we were led to believe."

A clatter at the back of the house distracted their attention. Two footmen opened wide the rear doors of the manor. Lady Alameda bustled out on Jerome's arm. Beside her came Lady Tricot with Sir Daniel at her side. Following the matrons, a cavalcade of servants poured out of the doorway, rolling carts of food, and carrying tables and chairs down the steps and out onto the grass in front of the gazebo.

"Daniel? Here?" Alex shook his head. He wondered if he'd gone to sleep on his horse, fallen off and hit his head. He was, perhaps, lying in a culvert at this very moment bleeding to death. *This* outlandish torment must be his dying dream. He groaned.

"Of course your brother is here, Mr. Braeburn." Lady Alameda approached him, smiling as if it were the most expected thing in the world that they should all be gathering on Lady Tricot's lawn. "Where else would a doting fiancé be, but dancing attendance on his intended? He's been engaging Muriel, Lady Tricot, in a riveting discussion concerning what fertilizer is best to use on leeks. And which is best for radishes."

Alex's mouth dropped for an instant. "He's engaged to Lady Tricot?"

Daniel stopped talking long enough to look aghast at his errant sibling.

Lady Tricot guffawed heartily. "My husband might have ought to say about that."

Lady Alameda rapped Alex on the arm with her fan. "No, silly boy. To our Willa, of course."

"Willa? No. He can't. Doesn't have to. It's I. I ruined her. It's my—"

"Mercy, I pray you." Lady Alameda put her hands to her ears. You're not going to prose on about 'duty' again are you? Frankly, I would rather sit through another discussion of fertilizers."

"But . . . I ruined her."

Jerome tut-tutted. "Nooo. I shouldn't think so. A simple carriage ride with an old family friend. Nothing untoward about that."

"No? I kissed her."

"Well, of course, you did, my boy. A brotherly peck on the cheek. Certainly not ruination."

"You didn't seem to think so yesterday."

Jerome sniffed. "Oh, well, yesterday I didn't have all the facts of the matter."

"And, I suppose, she"—Alex thrust his finger in the meddling countess's direction—"spooned up all the facts into a palatable little custard, did she?"

Jerome steepled his fingers and rocked a bit on his heels, looking like a black bell in his cassock. "A logical conclusion. My aunt merely explained all the nuances, that's all. A simple kiss between friends."

Lady Alameda smiled evenly, mischievously, a cobra biding her time for just the right moment to spit. "Yes, and now, be happy. Sir Daniel can marry our Willa, and they'll all retire to St. Cleve to live long and tedious lives." She smiled broadly.

"Just so." Jerome nodded, eyeing the trays of fruit and bowls of clotted cream the servants were laying out on the table.

"Tedious day all round." Harry toddled off to a bench under a nearby willow and plunked down. "Devilish tired. Wake me when nuncheon is served."

"Have you all gone mad?" Alex demanded. "It was a great deal more than a simple kiss between friends. Tell them, Willa!"

Willa tilted her head to the side and smiled genially. "Yes. Apart from Jerome springing the door open, it was the most wonderful night of my life. I shall treasure the memory forever."

Jerome shrugged. "There you are. Nothing to it." He rubbed his hands together as a footman laid out a full platter of sliced ham.

"Lunatics, one and all! What must I do? Ruin her right her in front of you? Very well—"

Alex grabbed Willa by the shoulders and kissed her. He meant for it to be a blunt, shocking kiss, not one for pleasure, a business kiss. Get the job done. But her mouth came to his willingly, spurring warmth he hadn't expected. Well, why shouldn't he enjoy it? Might alarm the idiots all the more. He kissed her until he almost forgot to breathe. She was flushed when he stopped, dazed, she faltered in her balance. He held her for a moment. "Forgive me, my dear. Had to be done."

In a booming voice he announced to everyone within earshot, "There! I have properly compromised her. Now, she has no choice but to marry me."

"Hhmm." Lady Alameda contemplated them, tapping her cheek with her fan. "Must she? I don't know. Muriel, what do you think?"

Lady Tricot shrugged. "I doubt it. No. Seen my dear old Godfrey kiss his horse with more warmth than that." She turned back to Daniel and continued their discussion of radishes.

Harry had lain down on the bench under the willow tree and laced his fingers across his belly. "Gel can't be compromised. We're all here chaperoning."

Alfreda and Tournsby made no comment. They sat deep within the gazebo, engrossed in Lord Byron's *Verses For All Occasions.*

Lady Alameda alone seemed intent upon the situation. "Do you wish to be forced into marriage, Mr. Braeburn?"

Alex frowned at her.

She bore down on him. "If we did relent, where would you keep a wife? Rented rooms in Blackfriars? Unsuitable for a young lady. Wouldn't you say, Jerome?" Lady Alameda nudged the vicar.

"Eh? What's that?" With visible reluctance Jerome turned his attention away from blueberry muffins and mince pies. "Blackfriars? Wouldn't know. I expect Willa could be happy nearly anywhere. Reform the entire neighborhood, knowing her."

Alex squared his shoulders. "Don't be absurd. I wouldn't expect her to live in Blackfriars. Sent my solicitor with an offer for the Ridley farm, day before yesterday. But see here, this isn't how I planned any of this."

"*You* planned?" Lady Alameda grinned widely.

He flexed the muscles in his jaw. So, she thought she'd run him aground, did she. Alex reached for Willa's hand. It didn't matter what the mad countess thought, he knew better. This was a thing far beyond her machinations. He knew it, even if she did not.

"Come." He pulled Willa apart from the others. When they'd walked a stone's toss away, he pulled her hands to his lips. "I know you think I am the worst kind of man—"

She started to protest, but he laid his finger against her lips.

"The truth is, I was a blind man, wandering aimlessly through London, through my life, until I met you. Life has never been the same since that one mistaken kiss. Now, I know exactly what I want. I want what Darley has. Children. A home. I want to be surrounded by the people I love." He glanced up the hill at the hapless conglomeration of their friends and family. "Even if half of them are completely balmy."

She smiled, and he couldn't resist brushing his fingers through her wildly curling hair.

She nodded.

He pressed his suit, holding her chin in his hand. "I know you imagine I've a harem, or scores of women secreted away. But I don't. There's only one woman I want. Willa, I love you. I think I knew it the day you walked down those vicarage stairs in that ridiculous shepherdess dress. I just didn't know what to do about it. Answer me, dearest. Do you think you could bear to spend the rest of your life with a man like me? A scapegrace? A prodigal? Do say something. What is it, my love? Your glasses are all spotted up—"

Willa couldn't see a thing.

Dratted tears. His face had become a watercolor blur. All the world washed into streams of color and puddles of soft sounds. No matter. She didn't need to see. More reliable senses took over, the ones that were able to sort through the incalculable, reach decisions without a balance sheet of figures dictating the answer.

She threw her arms around his neck and somewhere, in between sobs, he found her mouth and began to complete her happiness with unmistakable kisses.

AUTHOR'S NOTE

Shakespeare wrote the very first romantic comedies: *Midsummer Night's Dream, Much Ado About Nothing,* and *The Taming of the Shrew.* After he died, during the next two hundred years, who wrote romantic comedy? Oh, there were romances, Gothic and horror, certainly, but comedy? Not any that this student of literature can find.

Jane Austen was a genius. If she made a mistake it was in calling her books "Comedies of Manners." True, manners played a comedic role in her plots, but these stories were funny on many other levels. Her books ought to be credited for being the forerunners of Romantic Comedy.

I'd love to hear your opinion: www.KathleenBaldwin.com

More Regency Romance From Zebra

__**A Daring Courtship** by Valerie King	0-8217-7483-2	**$4.99**US/**$6.99**CAN
__**A Proper Mistress** by Shannon Donnelly	0-8217-7410-7	**$4.99**US/**$6.99**CAN
__**A Viscount for Christmas** by Catherine Blair	0-8217-7552-9	**$4.99**US/**$6.99**CAN
__**Lady Caraway's Cloak** by Hayley Ann Solomon	0-8217-7554-5	**$4.99**US/**$6.99**CAN
__**Lord Sandhurst's Surprise** by Maria Greene	0-8217-7524-3	**$4.99**US/**$6.99**CAN
__**Mr. Jeffries and the Jilt** by Joy Reed	0-8217-7477-8	**$4.99**US/**$6.99**CAN
__**My Darling Coquette** by Valerie King	0-8217-7484-0	**$4.99**US/**$6.99**CAN
__**The Artful Miss Irvine** by Jennifer Malin	0-8217-7460-3	**$4.99**US/**$6.99**CAN
__**The Reluctant Rake** by Jeanne Savery	0-8217-7567-7	**$4.99**US/**$6.99**CAN

Available Wherever Books Are Sold!

Visit our website at **www.kensingtonbooks.com.**

More Historical Romance From

Jo Ann Ferguson

Title	ISBN	Price
__A Christmas Bride	0-8217-6760-7	$4.99US/$6.99CAN
__His Lady Midnight	0-8217-6863-8	$4.99US/$6.99CAN
__A Guardian's Angel	0-8217-7174-4	$4.99US/$6.99CAN
__His Unexpected Bride	0-8217-7175-2	$4.99US/$6.99CAN
__A Rather Necessary End	0-8217-7176-0	$4.99US/$6.99CAN
__Grave Intentions	0-8217-7520-0	$4.99US/$6.99CAN
__Faire Game	0-8217-7521-9	$4.99US/$6.99CAN
__A Sister's Quest	0-8217-6788-7	$5.50US/$7.50CAN
__Moonlight on Water	0-8217-7310-0	$5.99US/$7.99CAN

Available Wherever Books Are Sold!

Visit our website at **www.kensingtonbooks.com.**

Discover the Romances of

Hannah Howell

My Valiant Knight	0-8217-5186-7	$5.50US/$7.00CAN
Only for You	0-8217-5943-4	$5.99US/$7.50CAN
Unconquered	0-8217-5417-3	$5.99US/$7.50CAN
A Taste of Fire	0-8217-7133-7	$5.99US/$7.50CAN
A Stockingful of Joy	0-8217-6754-2	$5.99US/$7.50CAN
Highland Destiny	0-8217-5921-3	$5.99US/$7.50CAN
Highland Honor	0-8217-6095-5	$5.99US/$7.50CAN
Highland Promise	0-8217-6254-0	$5.99US/$7.50CAN
Highland Vow	0-8217-6614-7	$5.99US/$7.50CAN
Highland Knight	0-8217-6817-4	$5.99US/$7.50CAN
Highland Hearts	0-8217-6925-1	$5.99US/$7.50CAN
Highland Bride	0-8217-7397-6	$6.50US/$8.99CAN
Highland Angel	0-8217-7426-3	$6.50US/$8.99CAN

Available Wherever Books Are Sold!

Visit our website at **www.kensingtonbooks.com.**

Embrace the Romance of

Shannon Drake

__**Knight Triumphant**
0-8217-6928-6 $6.99US/$9.99CAN

__**Seize the Dawn**
0-8217-6773-9 $6.99US/$8.99CAN

__**Come the Morning**
0-8217-6471-3 $6.99US/$8.99CAN

__**Conquer the Night**
0-8217-6639-2 $6.99US/$8.99CAN

__**Blue Heaven, Black Night**
0-8217-5982-5 $6.50US/$8.00CAN

__**The King's Pleasure**
0-8217-5857-8 $6.50US/$8.00CAN

Available Wherever Books Are Sold!

Visit our website at **www.kensingtonbooks.com.**

Celebrate Romance With One of Today's Hottest Authors

Amanda Scott

__Border Fire
0-8217-6586-8 $5.99US/$7.99CAN

__Border Storm
0-8217-6762-3 $5.99US/$7.99CAN

__Dangerous Lady
0-8217-6113-7 $5.99US/$7.50CAN

__Highland Fling
0-8217-5816-0 $5.99US/$7.50CAN

__Highland Spirits
0-8217-6343-1 $5.99US/$7.99CAN

__Highland Treasure
0-8217-5860-8 $5.99US/$7.50CAN

Available Wherever Books Are Sold!

Visit our website at **www.kensingtonbooks.com.**